Philip Boles

A native of Toledo, Ohio, **Philana Marie Boles** has a B.F.A. in creative writing and theater from Bowling Green State University. Prior to the release of her debut novel, *Blame It on Eve,* she lived in New York City, where she worked in the development office of Spike Lee's 40 Acres & A Mule Filmworks and then as an assistant to the director of media relations at *Glamour* magazine. Besides the blessing of being both a writer and spokenword artist, her favorite gig has been working as a substitute teacher, mentoring youth along the way. Her next novel (for young-adult readers) will be released in the fall.

Please pay a visit to Philana Marie Boles's Web site at www.pmarie.com.

in the paint

ALSO BY

PHILANA MARIE BOLES

Blame It on Eve

in the

a novel

paint

Philana Marie Boles

Amistad
An Imprint of HarperCollins Publishers

IN THE PAINT. Copyright © 2005 by Philana Marie Boles. Reading group guide copyright © 2005 by HarperCollins Publishers. All rights reserved. Printed in the United States of America. No part of this book may be used or reproduced in any manner whatsoever without written permission except in the case of brief quotations embodied in critical articles and reviews. For information, address HarperCollins Publishers Inc., 10 East 53rd Street, New York, NY 10022.

HarperCollins books may be purchased for educational, business, or sales promotional use. For information, please write: Special Markets Department, HarperCollins Publishers Inc., 10 East 53rd Street, New York, NY 10022.

FIRST EDITION

Designed by Kate Nichols

Printed on acid-free paper

Library of Congress Cataloging-in-Publication Data

Boles, Philana Marie.
    In the paint : a novel / Philana Marie Boles.—1st ed.
        p. cm.
    ISBN 0-06-057822-X (acid-free paper)
    1. Women painters—Fiction. 2. African Americans—Fiction.
3. Basketball players—Fiction. I. Title.

    PS3602.O653I5 2004
    813'.6—dc22

                                                    2004055129

---

05 06 07 08 09 BVG/RRD 10 9 8 7 6 5 4 3 2 1

for my cousins,

Liz Thompson, who made New York home,

and Bobby McCray,

who was absolutely right about circles

contents

acknowledgments

To God be the glory. I thank Him for my parents, Philip and Patricia, and for my sister Ginger, all of whom, for some incredible reason, still continue to put up with me, despite my starry-eyed and wacky ways. I thank Him also for my niece Jada, who keeps me laughing. I love you all.

Mel, the journey to publication always starts with you, with your stamp of faith and approval, and for that I am so grateful. Thank you also to Eric Lupfer, for your support and assistance.

This book is in so many ways the result of Kelli Martin, my editor. You always know the right questions to ask, the thought-inspiring comments and suggestions to make, leading us from a *whew-my-goodness* first draft a long while ago, to this. I appreciate your faith, encouragement, patience, and awesome gift of insight—including a title that "won."

My sincere appreciation also goes to the Amistad team at HarperCollins: Dawn Davis, editorial director; Rockelle Henderson, marketing director; John Jusino, managing editor; and Laura Blost, art designer.

Love to all my family! Love to my friends. Love to my readers. A special thank-you, for reasons they know, goes to Mrs. Christina Rode, Mrs. Rena Shuler, Mrs. Prudy Stone, Mr. and Mrs. F. Scott and Diane Regan, Ms. Kamia Strong, Mrs. Jane Charette, and M. W.—wherever he is. And a big up to my kids at SHS in Toledo. "Miss B." will never forget you. Be good.

in the paint

one

a woman laughing

Just for now, Danni Blair let the brush rest inside the mayonnaise jar. She watched as the water's color changed from milky orange to smoggy gray. And then, being careful where she stepped, she crossed the psychedelic sea of stones surrounding her. Across the room, on top of the mantel, her cell phone was vibrating, calling her out of her flow, demanding her attention.

Danni's strokes had been possessed by inspiration, hurried and unrestrained. Her paintbrush had worked a mild red indentation onto the inside of her middle finger. Some of the stones she'd painted red, like aged bricks or a confident woman's lipstick. Others were blue, powder-soft like the house she grew up in. For a glitzy effect, a few were canary or fourteen-karat yellow, subtle reminders of the life she was determined to leave behind. Some she'd wanted to represent grass, the shade depending on her side of the fence at that point in her life. Emerald like days past. Brown like today.

She made it across the hardwood floor, flipped open the phone, and, because her fingers were damp and discolored, she cradled it with her shoulder.

"Hey," she answered.

Kizzy's voice was hyped. "It's me, girl," she said. "I'm downstairs. You ready?"

Was it noon already? Danni snatched the remote control and flicked the television on to channel 105, lobby surveillance for residents of the refurbished warehouse where she lived, and sure enough, Kizzy's corkscrew curls popped up on the screen. Her grin was exaggerated, and with only her index finger she was waving into the camera.

Danni twisted her lips, glanced around her makeshift studio, and considered. No stone could be left unpainted, and eventually that canvas, propped up against the exposed brick wall, stark white and untouched, would become the horizon behind the sea of stones. Danni took too long to answer, and Kizzy knew her well.

Kizzy's voice was playful but firm. "Hold up," she said. "It's a gorgeous Saturday afternoon, and there's no *way* you're gonna stay cooped up inside. Buzz me up."

Please. So they could crack an ice tray, pop open some cans of Diet Vernor's, and spend, at minimum, an hour on girl talk? No way. Danni tightened the sweatshirt that she'd tied around her waist, and went right over and started fastening closed the bottles of paint. It'd be nice to hang out with Kiz and everything, but please, Danni wanted to be *back* in an hour.

Plus, maybe exercising would be good for her creative flow, so Danni focused on that. It wasn't like Kizzy was gonna stop all of her pestering; each one of her messages had been more insistent than the twelve before. *Girl, are you coming to the gym today? Girl, you keep on, you know you're gonna grow handles. Girl, you know if you don't burn off more than you take in every week it's gonna show.*

As if an extra pound or two or, okay, actually it was seven and a half, meant that Danni was no longer fly. As if lying alone for the last two months meant that Danni had been propping up pillows on her own deathbed. Please. Two months without a man and Kizzy, on the other hand, probably would've been weeping, calling out to the heavens that she wasn't ready yet to have her toe tagged.

Her theory was that Danni just needed exercise, that working a bucket of sweat out of her body would somehow make her happy again. Bless Kizzy's heart, ever the optimist, gotta love her, but please.

"I just need to scrub my hands," Danni told her, "and then I'll be right down." Why keep putting off till tomorrow what you damn well know you're not gonna wanna do then, either?

It was sweltering outside, remarkably sunny, and the streets were bustling because of it. Kizzy's shiny red convertible was parked out front, and she was profiling in the rearview, fluffing out her curls, hardly looking like someone who needed to go work out. Kizzy, on the other hand, spent more time at Perpetual Fitness than she did at her own pad.

"What's hap-nin, girl." Kizzy's smile was radiant.

"Hey." Danni pulled on her designer shades and reclined back in the seat.

"I don't know about you"—Kizzy pulled out into the flow of traffic—"But I'm ready to work it out, because *I'm* trying to strike gold at that party tonight. I'm tryin' to look ultra-svelte in my new sundress."

Danni hummed her agreement. "Say *that* again." She made her seat belt click, pulled at her ponytail, and started popping on her Spearmint.

"Did you decide what you're gonna wear yet?"

Danni heard the initial beats of Janet Jackson's new cut coming from WJLB, and was thankful for the diversion. She hadn't even *considered* what she might wear to that party tonight, let alone decided. After just a few more beats, Danni felt her gloom lifting. She could always count on Janet to remind her of carefree days past, temporarily sending her right back up to that emotional high again. She reached over and tapped on that tiny green arrow until she could literally feel the bass. Once upon a time that's what Danni's life had been all about. Feeling stoked about life. Stoked about her man.

Danni and Kizzy let out a simultaneous *yeah* and began snapping their fingers to the groove. With good music, their hair blowing with the wind, and the sun beaming an afternoon spotlight down on them, they pushed up the John R freeway looking fly and all the way fantastic, but like the portraits she painted, the illusions that defined her work, there was more to Danni. Her lips were smiling, but her eyes could not tell that lie. Her shades were blocking more than the sun.

Kizzy yelled above the music, over the wind, her voice wild with excitement, "Just wait, girl. We're gonna tear it up at that party. It's over for the competition. We're killin' it."

. . .

Forty minutes later though, Danni was the one dying.

Kizzy was climbing her way to a glorious heaven on the StairMaster, humming some cheerful melody, but Danni, who hadn't exercised in two months, was frantically trying to get that oh-my-goodness-this-is-so-impossible look off of her face. On top of that, she had an audience.

On Saturdays, if you weren't there by noon, you got last selection of the machines, ended up being mobile mannequins for shoppers at that strip mall, and right now people were strolling past, peeking, watching, and flat-out staring into the window.

Danni looked down at those big red digital numbers in front of her.

She *still* had another mile to go.

She hated that machine.

She hated Perpetual Fitness.

She hated people who smiled while they worked out.

And, more than anything, she *liked* being a size twelve.

She loved her hips. *Men* loved them. Please. Danni Blair was stacked like a grown woman should be. She was Catherine Zeta-Jones dipped in cocoa, au naturel and proud. She could give a damn about a six-pack. She should have gone next door.

She could have just had a peppermint-patty latte, a *Detroit Free Press,* a copy of *Newsweek,* and a corner table in a place where introspection and quality conversation held more weight than any barbells, a spot where timeless jazz whispered symphonic caresses throughout, where steamed coffee was the aroma.

But *nooo* . . .

The thick humidity and locker-room stench was consuming what limited breath she had left. And that stupid high-spirited teenage pop tune of the moment was deafening.

Men with broad upper bodies and legs like chickens were strutting around in tight, booty-hugging shorts, looking like Popeye after a can of spinach. Women were prancing about, looking primed for the cover of a fitness magazine, or like they were determined to begin their New Year's resolutions, never mind that it was already June.

Danni felt nauseous.

And damn it, her shins were on fire.

She needed to go to the restroom.

She had a headache.

She had a phone call to make, lint balls to pick.

She heard Kizzy gasp, and hoped for an emergency.

But Kizzy's eyes were wide, and she was smiling. "Look, look, look," she said.

Kizzy's radar was always on full alert, so considering the wild excitement on her face and the way her head was bobbing repeated nods at the window, it was obvious that a big-money baller had been detected. Twenty-five minutes on the StairMaster, and *now* Kizzy was out of breath.

Danni hated to brave that big clear glass in front of her, but she put on her who-gives-a-shit face and looked out. And she heard *herself* gasp.

"Just look at this." Kizzy's voice was low and breathless. "It's fate, girl. Has to be."

Now Danni actually *wanted* to run.

And of course, the buzz started up behind them.

"Is that . . . ?"

"Dallas Laylock!"

"Where?"

"*Who?*"

"Hoops for the Pistons, you know . . ."

"WHERE?"

"Outside. Right there."

"*Is that really him?*"

"Yup."

"Are you sure?"

"It is. Oh my goodness . . ."

"He looks taller on TV."

"In the flesh. That's really him. I'll be damned."

Danni imagined how she must've looked, sweaty, huffing,

puffing, a damn window distraction, and started pleading with the universe. *Please don't let him look this way. Please don't let him look this way. Please do not let him look this way.*

"He might look over here," Kizzy said. "Let's wave if he does."

Wearing long denim shorts, a black shirt with no sleeves to show off his black-panther tattoo, he had a heavy platinum rope necklace around his neck, and his oversize black ball cap was twisted to the side. Hoop dreams had rescued him from a life on the streets, had arranged for him a broadened view of the world, but Dallas Laylock was always gonna represent. He was down and dirty in a league where style was reigning king, an encore bad boy for the Pistons and hell-bent on looking like it.

He was sipping an iced coffee, had a newspaper tucked under his other arm, and he must've gotten that spooky feeling you get when someone is watching you, because he looked in their direction. Right at Danni. And she winced.

Great. Great. Great. Thank you so much, universe, for listening. Really. Thanks a whole lot.

His glance lingered, a cautionary pause before proceeding, and then a what's-up nod. He was unable to resist a nervous smile.

But Danni was strong, didn't smile back just yet. Thanks to him, her game had improved. She had a shitload of a defense that she was never again gonna pass to the wind. Please. What the hell ever. Wasn't no smile of his gonna buck her knees.

In exchange for his wow-it's-so-good-to-see-you smile, Danni extended an unquestionable rejection, a phony grin that she dropped real quick. Hey, why should she feel it necessary to be polite, just because *he'd* had the gall to put on a happy face?

For too long Danni had been charmed by that very same unbelievably magnetic sexy smile, foolishly thinking that *she* could keep that gleam in his eyes. For two years she'd actually thought that keeping her skin pampered and flawless, her body thick and toned, her baby-fine hair reinforced by a Hollywood weave would keep Dallas pressing strong for her. She'd been his cheerleader when she needed to be, his personal reality checker when necessary, all the while holding down her oh-so-sweet and oh-so-understanding girlfriend role, believing that their relationship would overcome the infamous two-year itch. Please. He still started scratching like he had a bad case of poison ivy. Two weeks after their two-year milestone, as a matter of fact, on a Saturday morning, in the kitchen, he junk-piled her.

He'd been pouring Pedigree into his rottweiler's dish, didn't even look up from the pebbles, didn't even wait for them to stop crackling against the stainless steel before he told her that they needed to talk. Danni finished loading the dishwasher, waited for him to stop pouring, and asked him what about. His shoulders shrugged and he sort of huffed. Or was that a sigh? Whatever it was, Danni could tell that he'd been doing some thinking, a *lot* of contemplating, and that the verdict was now in.

About what, she repeated in an even-tempered tone, and then she cleared her throat, her mind frantically trying to muzzle her instincts. This was not good, this was *not* good. He wasn't looking at her. If ever Dallas Laylock was going to propose marriage, being the sexy-eyed romantic brotha that he was, he would definitely be looking at her. He was down on one knee, but only to feed the dog. This definitely was not the proposal that Danni had been fantasizing about. She lifted her chin and awaited the blow. *What's up,* she said and felt her teeth clench.

Just some space, he suggested. That was all. He had too much on his mind, not that this had anything to do with her. He needed to focus on the duration of the season, on making the play-offs. He needed to clear his mind, figure some shit out, and he didn't want her to get hurt in the meantime. This was comical. As if getting the pink slip from the man she loved didn't feel the same as having a hammer whammed upside her head. Like *that* didn't hurt.

Still, she was intent on keeping her composure, on playing the cool, calm, confident, and diplomatic role. Danni asked him if there was something he wasn't telling her. Was there someone else, she wanted to know. Was he serious about all this?

With his back still facing her, his eyes still looking down into the dish, now full to the rim, each of Dallas's replies sounded as if his lawyers had prepped him, not at all binding, and full of loopholes. Not really, he said. Yes and no, he shrugged. He wasn't sure if it was all *that* serious, but he definitely meant what he said.

Huh?

When T-Bone galloped into the kitchen and forced Dallas out of the way, Dallas finally had to stand up, and then he turned around. But he checked out his fingernails for a long while before he finally faced her.

Danni's eyes spoke because her mouth would not, could not. Hadn't they just "happily celebrated" their two-year anniversary? Hadn't they been intimate, right upstairs in his king-size waterbed, just two nights ago? Couldn't he have at least had the decency to stop making love to her for a while *before* he came at her with this we-need-to-talk bullshit? Damn. Danni just looked away.

But then panic lunged up from her gut and grabbed hold of her throat, squeezing until her eyes felt strained. Unbelievable. Dallas was actually breaking up with her.

There was someone else. Had to be. Her thoughts were in a whirlwind. What the hell was this? And *where* was all this coming from? All that she'd put up with? Just to have things end? Like *this*? Two years, and Danni wasn't going to be Mrs. Dallas Laylock? What? Someone *else* was going to someday give birth to Dallas Jr.? *Ebony* magazine was going to feature Dallas Laylock and someone *else* in their annual "This Year's Hottest Weddings"?

Mind over matter, mind over matter, she kept telling herself. She concentrated on listening to T-Bone crunch his food. The swans were only humming, wasn't like this was the song. Wasn't like Dallas had just said that he never wanted to see her again. He hadn't asked for much. It was a simple request. A little space, that was all. Never one to be needy, Danni could handle that. Most definitely. Sure.

She turned back to face him and waited for his eyes to meet hers again. As best she could, she lifted the sides of her lips, and shrugged. Under no circumstances would she look hurt. *Ever*. And she would not let her panic show. Not even if it did feel like a straw has just come out from the sky and was sucking all of the air out of the earth. Danni could still breathe. All she had to do was remember to do so. Inhale. Exhale. Inhale. Exhale.

Maybe he'd just gotten a little scared. There wasn't a playa alive who didn't feel the urge to back up a little once he felt a love that was real, right? That's what Kizzy had always said, anyhow. And what was that old saying? If you love something, let it go, if it comes back to you . . .

Danni told Dallas to go on, handle his business, do his thing, take all the space he needed. For the umpteenth time in their relationship, she told him that she loved him enough to respect whatever it was he was going through. The tension on his face eased, a gentle kiss on her cheek, and he told her thanks, that he really appreciated that.

But days passed and he kept acting shady.

A month later, he was behaving like a damn lunar eclipse.

But just wait, Kizzy had assured Danni. Play it breezy. Don't sweat it. Be patient. The minute you put pressure on him, you're gonna push him away. A man can only sleep so long before he gets tired. He'll wake up. He'll remember who's been down there for him for two years. Just sit back, stay fly, and wait.

And so, very impatiently, Danni had been doing so.

But now that almost two *months* had gone by? Please. Danni

was supposed to just jump up and click her heels in the air just because she happened to run into him? Just act like she didn't mind being left on hold for so long, being left on hold *period*.

Just look at him, smiling at her from outside the window, fronting like seeing her had just put the icing on his fabulous afternoon. He glimpsed down, then back up, and the side of his lip curled up into a naughty smirk. Danni peeked down to see what it was that had him tripping.

Thanks to the treadmill, her breasts were bobbing up and down, looking like a pair of hyperactive speed bags. It was pitiful. Just great. So absolutely great.

Danni eased one hand off of the bar, reached down until she felt the bottom of her T-shirt, and grabbed hold and tugged. And in her very next gasp for breath, she was ticked. Who did he think he was, just freely checking out her goods like that? And *why* was he still laughing?

He finally looked away, and Danni noticed the long cord hanging from his ear. Oh. So the joke had come from his cell phone.

Kizzy was completely bugging out. "He saw you girl," she said, all goo-goo-eyed and animated. Then, as if Dallas could actually hear them through the thick glass, Kizzy whispered, "Wanna go say hi?"

"No," Danni snapped. *"No,"* she said again.

"But, girl . . . I mean, did you see the way he smiled when he saw you?"

"Oh, well," Danni replied. *"Oh well,"* she said again.

"I think you should at least go say what's up."

"Please."

"At least wave."

"For what?"

"To show that you're not pressed," Kizzy recommended with an unspoken *duh*.

Even if she wanted to, just to be polite, Danni knew she couldn't. One hand was holding down her breasts, and the other was holding on to the bar, and if she let go, *something* was going to be out of control, and *nothing* was going to be out of control, not ever. Never, never, never again.

And her foot missed the belt.

She kicked the side like she was taking off on a scooter.

Mind over matter. Mind over matter.

Her mind did *not* overcome the matter.

Without her consent, her other foot went right up along with the belt and her legs slid into doing the splits. Danni had to plaster a grip on that bar like there was a ninety-foot drop below her. She ended up with her chin resting on her knuckles. She wanted to cry.

Oh. So Perpetual's ceilings were fuchsia. Good to know.

It was a battle, but with a few quick movements, though her legs looked like Wilma Flintstone's taking off in a car, Danni used every muscle she could to pull herself back up, to stand erect again.

She started humming that Culture Club song she used to love back in the eighties. *Ain't nothing gonna break my stride. Oh, no . . . I've got to keep on moving.* But in order to catch back up with the pace of the belt, she *had* to put both hands on the bar. She hung her head, checked on her breasts.

Bong. Bong. Bong.

Why? Why? Why?

Kizzy asked, "Are you all right, girl?"

And then a voice from behind them chimed in, "Miss, are you okay?"

"Everybody, I'm fine," Danni announced. "Thanks. I'm okay." She watched the tips of her Reeboks and whispered, "Kiz, please tell me he's not still looking. Tell me he didn't see that. For once in our lives, I need you to lie to me."

But Kizzy was too weak with laughter to speak.

Danni was also unsuccessful in trying to maintain a straight face, and ended up releasing a chuckle herself. Hey, could've been worse, right?

Wrong. What could possibly be any worse than damn near collapsing flat on your back after just one smile from your ex-boyfriend, and him seeing you do so?

"Kizzy, come on," Danni pleaded. "We're talking potential devastation here. Is he looking or not?"

"Okay, okay." Kizzy finally wiped the tears of laughter from her eyes. "His back is turned. The coast is cool."

Sure enough, Dallas was looking out into the sea of cars, obviously still talking to the comedian.

"Ain't it something, girl," Kizzy started up again. "How you can just *tell* a man with money? The way they walk . . ." She was far off in a zone somewhere. "The way they can make simple clothes, like even a T-shirt and a pair of denim shorts look so damn runway-ish?"

Danni smacked the big red emergency stop button, and was on the floor before the thing had even come to a complete stop. The same area that had been deserted a little while ago was alert now, purring with *oohs, aahhs,* and *uums.*

One of the chicks standing there, wide-eyed and spandex-tailed, looked like her mission in life was to star in a rap video. Danni got her attention, gestured with a nod at the treadmill that she'd just abandoned. "Take mine," she told her.

"Really?"

The girl look completely baffled, like Danni had just given her a blank check, a pen, and told her to get happy or something. Please.

Dallas Laylock might've looked all bright, sparkly, and wonderful from afar, but up close he was heat. *Painful* heat. So what if he could be seen on Sportscenter? Had had a cameo in that Spike Lee flick? So what if he *had* been Danni's for two years?

So what if he was a power forward who governed the floor, manipulated the ball, and protected the basket like a machine programmed to do so? So what if he had a mean-ass behind-the-back pass? Dallas Laylock was even savvier on the social court. His *real* player skills were absolutely wretched, and his selfishness, both on and off the court, were the main reason he wasn't wearing any rings.

Oh sure, he had let Danni run wild like a savage up in Somerset Collection, spending outright sinful amounts of money at Saks, Neiman Marcus, and Bebe. Yes, there had been the downpours of surprises, yes, he kept Danni always looking like not even a penny short of a dime, and *yes,* Danni had loved all of it. The fancy bracelets that made her wrists sparkle. Necklaces that did the same. Her feet arched by designers' names.

But Dallas Laylock was also obsessed with other things.

He was consumed with justifying his four-year, $98 million contract when commentators and the growing restless general public had begun to accuse him of being nothing more than a pistol, an intimidating game face with an outrageous dunk.

He lived for better stats in the paper, more dynamic clips on the news.

He had four cars. He wanted more.

He wanted *more* zeroes on his bank statements.

Danni had been there, done the sunburns. No thanks.

No more riding shotgun on Kizzy's voyages trying to conquer wealthy men just *because* they were wealthy. What was the point, just to ultimately sit around for two months waiting, bitching, whining, and complaining about how she'd gotten played? Tripping, because not only had she lost him, but in some ways she'd also lost *herself* in the process. Plenty of designer shit in the closet, a plethora of nuclear bomb—level sex memories, but please. None of that had never mattered to Danni before she met Dallas.

After putting herself on hold for two years, Danni was supposed to just wait for him to stop straddling the fence, could he live with her, could he live without her? Please. Whoops, there goes the buzzer. Time was up. Game was *ova.*

Kizzy was so gone by now that she hadn't even noticed that

Danni was no longer next to her. "Look at that," Danni heard Kizzy say. "A stallion. Money forever. Girl, I know you miss him. I *know* you still want that."

Danni looked over at spandex girl. "I'm finished," she told her. "Go right on ahead."

"Cool," the girl responded with a neck roll and a grin.

Danni could have corrected her, issued a warning. No, actually it's *hot,* she could have informed her. An inferno. A lake of fire. What hell probably burns like. But, hey, let her jump right on out there, reach on out and touch. Let her watch, too, feel it as the blisters rise up on the tips of her fingers after she does.

• • •

She folded her arms across her chest, and glared at the locker room door beyond which Kizzy was changing. Ten more seconds, and Danni was going in after her.

A soft and dumpy guy in sweats walked past, wiping his forehead and turning up a bottle of water. He noticed Danni, reversed, and stood close enough to smell her Tic Tac. She raised an eyebrow.

"Yes?" she said.

He massaged his gut like he was proud of it. "Just got through playing some racquetball," he said. "Ran a few laps . . . How 'bout yourself?"

"I'm waiting on someone," Danni replied.

"Who, the lil' cutie-pie I saw you come in with?"

"Excuse me?"

"Cute lil' curly-haired thing you came in with?"

"Oh," Danni said. "Right."

"I see her in here all the time," he explained.

"I'm sure. This place is her second home."

He considered Danni's face a little closer, *too* close, and said, "I know you from somewhere?"

Danni glanced back at the door, and tried real hard to ignore how close this man was. But she couldn't. "No," she eased away. "I don't think we've met."

"So, um"—he took a swig of his water—"Either one of ya'll single?"

Danni's laugh lingered. Was he serious? Wanting to see if he was, she read his face. He was. Definitely.

"Look here." He held out his palms in peace. "Two beautiful women, don't think I wasn't gonna at least ask. Figured I'd at least have a chance with one of ya'll. I ain't shamed."

Danni crunched on her Tic Tac.

He said, "So what's up?"

She folded her arms across her chest and started tapping her Reebok. "What's up with *what?*"

"Look-a-here," he said. "Ain't no *rang* on your finger, and wasn't one on hers neither. So, what's up? One of ya'll tryin' to holla?"

The nerve. The audacity. The total omission of tact.

His puffy hand was extended for her to shake. "Ben Brown," he said.

"Danni." She pretended not to notice.

"Short for Danielle?"

"No," she said. "Just Danni."

He licked his chops, added some bass to his voice. "So, *just Danni*, what's up?"

Ding-ding-ding. Time. That's what was up. He needed to go, and so did she. Danni zeroed in on the locker-room door.

"Wit' yo' fine self." He watched her walk away.

· · ·

Kizzy was putting the finishing touches on her face, perfectly made up to look natural. Her mascara, lip gloss, and lip liner were all still intact, had been before, during, and after her workout. "Hey girl," she said. "I'm almost ready." She blotted her lips and blew the air a kiss. "Umm," she said. "I just love this stuff. It's waterproof. See how it stayed?"

"Yeah, great," Danni replied. "Can I just have the keys? I think I'll wait in the car, if that's cool."

"You all right?"

Danni replied with a shrug. "Fine. Why?"

"Because, you know, once you get back in the routine, your body will readjust to—"

Danni tapped her knuckles on a locker. "I know," she said. "I just need some air."

But Kizzy saw the look on Danni's face. "Uh-oh," she said. "Talk to me. What's up?"

"Nothing."

"Naw, naw, girl. Come on."

"Let it go, Kiz. I said I'm cool."

"Something's up."

Danni shrugged. "Maybe it's being up inside this damn meat market again."

"Meat market?"

"It feels like a damn juke joint. Worse."

Kizzy brushed that off with a wave of her hand. "Girl . . ."

"Really," Danni said. "Some guy out there just asked about either of us at the same time, came right out and said it and everything, like we were two birds, a coin toss or something, like either one of us would suffice. 'Either one of ya'll single, tryin' to holla? Ain't no shame.'"

Kizzy cracked up laughing.

Danni shook her head. "Trifling, huh?"

"Was he cute?"

Danni sliced Kizzy a look, let it linger, and flared her nostrils. "And you ask me if he's *cute?*"

Kizzy laughed some more. "Well . . ."

"Unbelievable."

"Maybe he was nice, you know? Am I so wrong for wanting to see you with someone besides that damn paintbrush every night?"

"Someone," Danni corrected her. "Not just anyone."

"Well, of course I know *that,* but—"

"Plus," she said, "at least my brushes are loyal, stay true to the one who holds them."

Kizzy pulled a bottle of lotion from her gym bag. "And that's all good, but, you know, there's nothing wrong with a lit-tle . . ." She paused. "What am I talking about? Ain't nothing wrong with *a lot* of flirting."

"That brotha was flat-out tired. Um, so *no*."

Kizzy put her hands on her hips and posed. "He liked what he saw, girl. Ain't a damn thing wrong with that."

"Uh, can I get a 'hi, how are you?' I mean, whatever hap-pened to a little decency?"

Kizzy slathered some lotion on her well-defined arms. "I hear you, girl. But that fool might've had a good job for all you know, some real ends. You never know . . ."

Danni just shook her head, and sighed. "There you go."

"There I go where?"

"Nothing."

"Girl, what's *really* got you so tight?"

"Can I just have the keys?"

"Seeing Laylock got you bent?"

Danni rolled her eyes.

"Umm-hmm . . ." Kizzy said. "Keys my ass."

"Okay, I'm human," Danni admitted. "So yeah. I had a mo-ment. And so what. It passed. Just like our relationship."

"He was looking too good though, wasn't he?"

"Kiz, you know, I could've sworn that it was you who kept telling me how nice of a day it is outside."

"One hundred degrees *plus* since you saw him, I bet."

"Well." Danni ignored her. "I'd like to enjoy this beautiful day, alright?"

"Right, right . . ." Kizzy was nodding, still grinning.

"Dallas hasn't changed, and he's not going to. So please."

"Right, right . . ."

"And I am *not* that weak. What? Just because I happen to run into him, *whoops* there go the panties? Please. No explanation or nothing? Not this thong."

"Umm, hmm. Preach, sista, preach."

"All right," Danni snapped. "*Stop* cosigning when you know damn well you don't mean it."

Kizzy rolled her eyes with dramatic passion. "Look at you. That fool has you bent like a damn yoga position."

"Please."

"He was lookin' too happy when he saw you, girl. Like, ummm, *what*. I told you. Just be patient. He's gettin' ready to wake up."

"Please," Danni said. "I'm not dealin' with Dallas Laylock anymore. I do not miss the stress."

Kizzy was quiet for a minute, watching the floor and all that jazz, but in all sincerity, she shrugged. "It's like this, girl——"

"Kiz, no. Don't even go——"

"I've gotta say it. I'm sorry. Look, I know he hurt you, put your heart in a blender and held down all the buttons like you like to say, but okay, so what. You're strong. We came into this world equipped with resiliency. What?"

"And that makes it right? The fact that I can handle it?"

"Girl, no."

"Like I'm just gonna be here, waiting and willing, still wanting him. Please. It's *not* like he's the last of the stallions."

Kizzy fluffed out her curls. "True, true . . ."

"But what," Danni demanded. "I know one is coming."

Kizzy smiled. "Just, all I'm saying is that if he wants to talk, at least hear him out, let him spit it out, even if it's bullshit. Shoot, if nothing else get the closure you need. Deserve. And you *do* need that, girl."

"He has nothing to say to me."

"But what if he comes at you right?" Kizzy wrapped her towel around her neck. "You never know. . . . It could be your fairy tale. I saw the way he looked at you, girl."

"I am *not* driving in reverse. From now on, it's about me, myself, and my craft."

Kizzy shook her head, a sigh voicing her agreement. "I know that's right. Get back focused on your dreams, girl. But what if it doesn't have to be one or the other?"

Danni's voice was tired, barely audible. "How about if you just give your girl the keys?"

"Because if it was me? I'd be right out there in that parking lot, batting the hell out of this damn waterproof mascara. Drop my towel on purpose, making good and damn sure Dallas was looking before I did. Life is too long without good sex." Kizzy tossed Danni the keys. "Better wake up, girl."

• • •

His Hummer, black and chromed out, was parked two spaces over, and he was standing in the driver's-side doorway signing autographs, devouring every one of his groupies' verbal massages.

"Here you go." He handed one back her water bottle, now

anointed with his scrawl, and he looked over in the direction where Danni was walking. Their eyes met, but Danni looked away, concentrated instead on not chipping the paint, getting that damn key to go in. She heard the collective sounds of disappointed moans. And then she heard a door slam. Her heart flipped.

Okay. But maybe he'd gotten *in*to the car.

Maybe Danni would turn back around, and he'd be gone.

Footsteps, one hushed step at a time, grew closer, and closer, and closer. And then his hand, so strong, so firm, was on her waist. Seeing as how this made Danni freeze up like an ice glacier, she was of course unable to turn around.

His voice was soothing and deep. "I know you saw me," he said. "It's cool."

Why was she acting like this? She needed to buck up, play the strong role, not be affected by his presence, damn it.

"Actually," she replied with a quick jerk of her shoulders. "I did see you."

He pressed on her waist. "Got me standin' here talkin' to your ponytail and thangs . . ."

Determined to let him see how unruffled she was, Danni finally faced him. All six feet, all three of those inches were up there, so accessible, but so off limits. Even though his oversize ball cap was pulled down low on his face, Danni managed to find his eyes, clearly searching for communication with hers. Did she hate him?

She wanted to smile; after all, she *had* made love to this man for two years. Looking into his eyes made her feel as if the last time had been just last night. "Hey," she said, keeping her face emotionless.

He took her hand, palm down, into his, and while maintaining eye contact, he brought it to his lips. Danni refused to react, and Dallas noticed. His eyes, such restrained desire, expressed such heartfelt concern. "You all right?" he wanted to know.

"Oh, I'm cool," she said with ease. "It's a beautiful day."

His smile, so familiar, was playful and mischievous as he kissed her hand again.

Those lips. So . . .

Danni blinked, rebuked the rush of nostalgia.

He bit his bottom lip. "How've you been?"

She felt a twinge of skepticism. Maybe he was just being nice, just wanted to say hello. For old-times' sake. He'd seen her, didn't wanna be rude. Maybe he'd just wanted to make sure that she hadn't been hurt while flipping around on that treadmill. It was the sportsman in him, of course, to wonder about her ankle.

Could he tell how quick, how nervous, her heartbeats had become?

Could he sense that inside she was trembling, felt like crying?

Could he feel how her hand was growing moist? She eased it out of his, and slipped a cheerful mask on her face. "I'm doing great," she told him. "Real good, actually."

And, him just being Dallas, he glanced down at her breasts again. That naughty grin was back in full effect. He asked her, "And my girls?"

She folded her arms across her chest and wished that she had two words in big bold colors across the front of her T-shirt, NOW CELIBATE. Better yet, CELIBATE UNTIL CEREMONY. Wasn't no warm kiss on her hand gonna break her will, gonna make her just disregard everything. Please.

He said. "Saw you workin' it out in the window."

Danni glanced back at the gym. "Yeah. I, uh, hadn't been in a while."

"Why's that?"

"I've been busy."

He was hesitant, but said, "That right?"

"Busy, busy, busy," she said.

"Who with?"

"Oh, a lot of things . . ."

"Could've sworn I said *who*. What, I know 'em or somethin'? Lay it on me if I do."

"No," she said without flinching. "You don't know him."

His jaw muscles rippled, and he started chewing his gum slower and real hard. Danni enjoyed watching. That's right. Two bits. Four bits. Six bits. A dollar. Used to be your cheerleader, but now you gets no holla.

He scanned her eyes for some hint of a joke, for a no-I'm-just-kidding to come out of her mouth. He said, "Ya better be playin'."

Danni shrugged. "I'm not."

Please. Just because he was still charming, just because he kept the right edges rough, just because he had millions in the bank, just because he was Dallas Laylock . . . what? Danni couldn't move on? Is it so unbelievable that she couldn't have met someone else by now? She'd met him, hadn't she?

A female voice from behind them broke in. "Dallas?"

He frowned a tad, but looked back over his shoulder. "What up?"

An older lady was waiting politely, total awe on her face, and was holding a notepad and pencil.

Dallas extended one of his winning smiles. "How you doin'?"

She was struggling against her excitement, tickled by Dallas's smile. "My grandson," she said, "enjoys you so much. Could you make this out to him? He'd be *so* happy."

"Tell m'man to stay in school." Dallas took the pencil. "Be somebody. What's his name?"

She looked over at Danni and smiled. "Oh, I do. All the time. Every day. His name's Jamal Jackson, and he just turned twelve."

Dallas started writing. "Good deal," he said.

"He's usually out, running errands with me, you know, things like that. He'll be upset he wasn't with me today. Thank you."

Dallas offered a few incessant nods. "Be sure and tell him what I said, a'ight?"

She looked at the paper, and tightened her grip. "Will do," she said as she left.

Danni twirled the keys. Had places to go. Other things to do. "That was nice," she told him, her tone purposefully dry.

"For the kids, know what I'm sayin'?"

An annoyed expression, completely unintended, covered

Danni's face. Please. Just a few minutes ago he had been doing the same thing for the groupies. For the kids, Danni's ass. For anyone was more like it.

He noticed her mood shift. "What up?"

But Danni still had way too much pride to appear resentful. "Nothing," she replied.

He dropped his voice a little. "So, I can't even get a hug?"

She didn't bother with a reply, gave him a hell-no look instead. And he laughed.

"Ay." He wasn't affected in the least. "It's cool."

"It was good to see you, but—"

"Come rap with me for a minute, a'ight? I wanna holla at you real quick." He didn't even look to see if she was coming, just turned around and swaggered over to his truck.

Five minutes, Danni promised herself. By then Kizzy should be finished primping. By then maybe he would've spit enough of his bullshit to extinguish any and all lingering maybes. By then maybe Danni would have convinced him so tough that she'd moved on, that she had somebody else. Let *him* wonder for a twist.

• • •

The inside of his Hummer smelled of crisp pine. Dallas was always replacing the air fresheners hanging from the knob of his cigarette lighter, always wanted his cars to smell fresh. Remembering all of this made Danni feel warm inside, made her long for all of his endearing quirks. She surveyed his new ride. Wood-grain trimmings. Supple cream-leather interior.

CD changer. His initials, D.L., embroidered in mahogany on the dash and the floor mats.

"Nice," she said.

"Rides with authority." He started the ignition.

She reached for the door handle. "Don't think I'm leaving with you, because I'm not."

He moved his neck to a Trick Daddy beat. "Chill," he said. "Just tryin' to hear some music."

"Don't you dare pull off, Dallas, I swear."

He turned off the ignition. "All right, lemme stop, before you start wildin' out," he said.

"Thank you."

"So, what up? Life treating my baby right?"

She cleared her throat. Still, he was calling her baby, and *still* it gave her the tingles when he did.

"Better be," he added.

"*I'm* treating me right," she said. "I'm loving the skin I'm in, and I'm happy. How about that? Everything else I tune out."

He stared at her, a misty longing in his eyes.

"Don't start," she said.

He touched her hand. "Skin so soft . . ."

"It's not happening," she pulled her hand away.

He touched her face, gentle, too quick for her to react. "Can't never see my dimples anymore . . ."

"Well." She sighed. "Whose fault is that?"

He gave her knee a squeeze, and let his hand rest right there.

She reached down, and pulled it right off.

"My baby won't even let me touch her . . ."

"Nope."

He started to say something, but changed his mind. "I'm glad you're straight," he said. "On everything."

"I'm glad about that too," she replied. What did he think, that she'd be dazed and insane by now?

He took off his hat, scratched his head a bit, long enough for Danni to see that he needed a haircut. "What's up with the mini fro," she asked.

"Man," he said. "To hell with a cut. On everything. I'm 'bout to rock some cornrows." He pulled his hat back on and tugged on the brim. "You gon' braid my hair for me?"

"Why would I willingly help you to look even more thugged out?"

He shrugged. "You don't even care how I'm doin'?"

She looked out the passenger-side window, studied the skyline of Detroit, and though it didn't sound like it, she actually did want to know. "How have you been, Dallas?"

"Sick," he said without hesitation. "On everything."

Still stuck on stale, she replied, "Oh. Really?"

"Without my baby? Come on, man . . ."

"Well, you should be. And you can stop calling me 'baby.' "

She focused on the bridge to Canada, and started tapping the door handle. Tapping. Tapping. Tapping. It was a nervous habit of Danni's. And realizing how fidgety she was, she actually wondered if maybe this *could* all be fixed, if maybe he had just messed up, if maybe she *was* being too hard. He did still make her tap.

But in her very next blink she was back from orbit, was back in Detroit, back inside her smooth cocoa skin. She remembered all the nights that she'd stayed up wondering who was he with, was he okay, would she ever see him again. She remembered the fact that she hadn't heard from him in two months. That familiar stab of grief knew exactly where to find her chest, and did. Danni rumbled around in the pocket of her sweatpants for her Tic Tacs, and crunched on one as if it was Percocet.

"Dallas, just say what you need to say, all right? I've gotta get going."

"Let's go get somethin' to eat."

She shook her head. "Absolutely not. *No.*" She hadn't eaten since the bagel this morning. *Of course* she was hungry, felt famished, in fact, but hell no. She'd nibble on her own knuckles before she willingly left with him.

"Trippin'."

"I'm not."

"Sittin' all far away, like I've halitosis or somethin'."

"Well."

He patted the seat. "Come here."

"No."

"What, you hate me?"

"Nope." She shrugged. "Hey, I'm over it."

He choked on that, found that *real* funny. "Over it?"

She faced her opponent, was ready to go to verbal blows if necessary. *"Yes,"* she said. "Over it."

"See there. Always trippin'."

"I'm serious. Two tears in a bucket . . ."

He chuckled. "Just good for two, huh?"

"Actually, let me retract that, maybe just one and a half."

"Trippin'."

"I'm serious."

He touched her leg again. "Sure about that?"

She swatted his hand.

"Damn, girl."

"I'd swear under *oath*."

He laughed. "Yo." He smiled at his thoughts. "Remember when we used to just kick it? Make popcorn balls, virgin daiquiris when I was in season, just sit up in the crib and chill after a game." He pinched her cheek. "My baby was just ride or die. Ain't that right?"

She yawned on purpose. "Not your baby anymore . . ."

He squeezed her thigh. "Remember how you used to bite my neck?"

She reached to open the door. "Good-bye . . ."

He reached over and grabbed her hand, his grip Herculean. One finger at a time, he pulled her hand off the door handle. His voice a whisper now, "Hold up a minute, baby. We can't even just talk for a minute?"

Talk. For a minute. Like all it would take was a *minute* for him to possibly address the rip he'd left in her heart.

"Look," she told him. "I'm minding my own business, *and* I'm taking care of it. I know that might be impossible for you to believe, but I am. You're not my air, Dallas. I'm breathing fine without you. Hear me."

"Oh, I definitely hear what you sayin' . . ."

"Good."

His grin was calculating. "Over me, huh?"

"That's right."

He scrunched his nose and winked. "Let's go. Let's go get some grub."

She looked away. "Not a good idea."

Slight amusement in his voice, he said, "Scared you might enjoy yourself?"

"It's nice to see you, but no."

Now, with a grin in his voice, he said, "So let's kick it tonight. You're over me, right?"

"Please."

"You ain't gotta beg, baby."

"That's not what I meant, and you know it."

All jokes aside, he said, "Man, what's this fool's name? You dealin' with somebody."

She shrugged. "Maybe. Or *maybe* I'm just content with Danni. Ever thought about that?"

He squeezed her arm, another gesture he did not seem at all apprehensive about. "Some fool won't let my baby work out." He gave her arm another squeeze, harder this time. "Trying to keep my baby on lock."

She snatched her arm out from his grasp. "Please. You see I'm here."

"Saw those legs get weak when you saw me, too." He squeezed her thigh again.

She blushed, tried not to laugh. "Please."

He rubbed her leg. "Oh, but you're smilin' though. Miss me?"

She pushed his hand away again.

"So who's this fool? Must be a nerd, a damn couch potato or something, won't let you leave the damn house."

She smacked her lips. "No."

He reached in, tried to cup her breast in his hand, but she slapped him away before he was able. "Stop it," she said. "Would you?"

"I'm just sayin' what up to the girls . . ."

She looked him directly in his eyes. "Dallas, *stop it,*" she said. "I mean it."

He winked. "Real quick."

"See what I mean? See why I don't want to talk to you?"

"All right, all right." He touched her arm softly this time. "You know I'm just playin'. My baby ain't no freak."

She folded his arms across his chest. "Thank you. And *stop* calling me baby."

"Man, what's this fool's name, so I can run a check on his ass? Tryin' to handle my baby. Probably a punk. Probably got bad credit and shit."

Danni refused to laugh.

"All right then," he said. "Don't tell me. Three guesses, cool?"

She shrugged.

"He hoop?"

She rolled her eyes. "Please."

"What, he a lawyer, some shit like that?"

She blinked a few times. *"No."*

"All right," he said, really getting a kick out of this. "I know you're not dealin' with no broke-ass buster can't buy you shit. Lemme see . . ."

"What's *that* got to do with anything? I do work, *hello* . . ."

"Shit. And?"

She shook her head. "See. You don't even know me."

"I know you like quality shit. I know can't no broke muh-fucker handle that. What, you still at that glass bougie-looking joint?"

"ReveNations," she corrected him. "And, yes."

"You happy?"

"Very."

"Then so am I," he said. Then his face frowned up again. "And what you mean, I don't know you?"

"I know you *think* you do . . ."

"Trippin'. I know you've got a real cute laugh, a muh-fuckin' gorgeous-ass smile."

"Besides all that."

"Fly-ass dimples. Where they at?"

"People smile when they have a reason to."

"I hear what you sayin' . . ."

"So what else? You know so much."

"You and Kiz grew up together . . ."

"Okay . . ."

"She still out here cluckin'?"

"Kiz is *not* a chickenhead. So relax with all that."

"*Sheeeiiiit*. Like hell. Out here, lookin' for backers and shit."

Danni sighed, wasn't worth getting worked up about it. "I'm waiting on her now."

"Damn cluck," he laughed.

"At this point, I am ignoring you, Dallas."

"All right, now, lemme see, lemme see . . ."

"Can't think, can you? You think you know *soooo* much. Not everything, you don't."

He rubbed his hands together. "I know you don't move while you sleep, used to scare the shit out of me at first."

She fought the urge to smile, and won. "And?"

"I know you love them satin sheets."

She smacked her lips. "Please."

"I know mint chocolate chip is your favorite ice cream. I know you like it hard." He laughed heartily.

The audacity of him to keep making her face burn.

Seeing a smile rising in her eyes made him want to keep going. "Lemme see, lemme see. What else?"

"All right. That's good enough."

"Hold up a minute, now, hold up . . ."

"That's okay," she said. "You can stop now."

"I know you can't handle a Teena Marie song without gettin' hot, strokin' them nails all over my neck and shit."

She had to laugh a little. "I thought I just said that that's enough."

"Ah, what up, what up? I hear my baby's laugh comin'."

She relaxed her cheek muscles. "Please."

"I know you keep your toenails painted red 'cause you know I like 'em like that."

She sucked her cheeks in, succeeded in stopping the grin. "Actually that would be because *I* like 'em like that. Let's not get it twisted."

"I *bet*."

"Okay, I said you don't have to keep—"

"I know my baby's got a tattoo on the small of her back. I damn for sure know what the 'D' and the 'L' stand for."

"It's now a rose," she informed him. "And, please. The 'L' is a thorn now."

His smile was gone. "Aw, now that's fucked up."

"Yeah, well, so are a lot of things. Want specifics?"

"Come wit' it."

"Not hearing from you for two months? Oh, *real* fucked up."

"Shit's been crazy. I—"

"No. *That's* fucked up, Dallas."

"Shit, gotdamn," he said. "All right, all right."

She looked over at Kizzy's car. "For two whole years, thinking you're going somewhere with someone, then realizing that it was nothing more than a false start. Pretty fucked up."

He took a deep breath, didn't know what to say.

She attempted to sum everything up with some generic statement about it being nice to have seen him and for him to take care, but Dallas wasn't hearing it, kept right on pressing.

A palpable determination was in his voice now. "Still over at ReveNations . . ."

"Still trying to do my own thing eventually though."

He removed the plastic cup from the cup holder and sipped on what was left of his iced coffee. She watched as the cup sweated, one drip at a time, onto his hand, and waited as the silence trickled along with a similar delay.

He said. "I'm takin' you to lunch this week. Comin' to get you from work so we can spend the afternoon together, so we can talk."

"No-you're-not," she sang.

"It's time out. I—"

"Exactly. Time *out*."

"See there. Always trippin'. Oh, I'm takin' you to lunch."

That's when Danni peeped that look on his face, that all-too-familiar look from his game, the subdued determination of a brotha clearly thinking *might not getcha now, but I'll getcha later*. It was the same look he gave her the night they met.

It was at the Detroit Music Fest, and Kizzy had just gotten Dallas's autograph. He then held his hand out to Danni, for something of hers to sign next, but she didn't have anything. It wasn't that she didn't dig basketball, that she wasn't flattered to meet him, but what was the point? Just to prove to people like, *look* Dallas Laylock wrote his name for me. Danni was more pumped about hearing Maze perform.

Dallas checked Danni out a bit, and asked her, "So, what's your name, sweetheart?"

"I'm just here for the concert," she replied, "but it's Danni." She flicked the hair off her shoulder, and offered her usual explanation when he inquired about her name.

He tilted his head, his thick eyebrows hunching together. "Oh yeah?"

"Ma wanted to name me after Daniel, you know the whole lion's den thing, how God delivered Daniel, but she liked Danni better than Danielle."

He thought for a moment before he commented further. "Yeah. I guess God looked out for old Daniel, huh?"

"I need him to look out for me too," she replied with a soft smile.

His eyebrows lifted, illustrating his interest, noticing her dimples. "That right?"

She had fun with her response. "Lion's jaws all out here in this world. All on the prowl. All in the clubs. Grocery stores. Church. Everywhere." She laughed some more. "Just licking their chops, just eager for the next piece of meat to devour. You think I want to be somebody's meal?"

He was humored, his face glowing with a smile. And he agreed. "I feel that."

"It's different when you're the meat though," she clarified.

His nod was insistent. "I feel that. And, uh, I'm definitely feelin' that smile."

"Thank you . . ."

"Yeah . . . oh yeah."

"And you know—" She joked some more, wanted to keep down her flutters. "I'll be damned if somebody's gonna put me on a plate. Sop me up with a damn buttermilk biscuit."

Interest in his eyes, he said, "You ain't nothing to play with, huh?" He reached down and felt her arm, a gesture he did not

seem at all apprehensive about, and was visibly stunned by
what he felt, what her silk blazer was withholding. He gave it
another squeeze, harder this time, and Danni was taken aback,
couldn't believe that he'd actually reached down and touched
her like that. Twice. Like she was a piece of fruit he was considering at the market. Like just because he was Dallas Laylock
he had it like that. And she also couldn't believe that she'd allowed him to do so.

He said, "I would tease you about being a tough girl, but I
see that wouldn't be a joke. Shit. I mean gotdamn."

"I paint," she explained.

"I'm sayin', what, Laila Picasso and shit?" He folded his arms
across his chest, appeared ready to just kick back and rap for a
while. "Paint what?"

"Whatever I feel."

"I think artist, I think turquoise jewelry and bell bottoms.
You standin' here looking like you push a Jag. Rockin' the silk
suit . . ."

Misclassification had always been an issue for Danni. She
had always been a square peg surrounded by holes. Her style
was *Vogue* while the buppies she worked with dressed in ethnic
garb, burned incense in their offices. Yet, she had to turn
C-SPAN off when Kizzy came over, hurry up and flick it to the
E! channel. But still, Danni had a few too many Adam Sandler
and Chris Tucker DVDs in her collection to converse about the
aesthetics of film with the folks who did.

Danni was spiritual, definitely believed in a higher power,
but she wasn't down with being a member of Ma's seven-

hundred-member cult. She dug the whole feminist movement, she herself considering the word *obey* to be a four-letter word, but she was actually cool with it if a man wanted to cut the grass and fix the cars while she planted the flowers. In high school, while all the other girls had lunch over giddy, boy-crazy talk, Danni chose to sit outside on the lawn with her sketchbook, just as happy and unaware of anything in the world besides what she was drawing. The girl whom everybody knew but nobody bothered to know—*that* was Danni.

She told him, "People think they can take one look at me and have me pinned, but please. I'm not so obvious."

With every one of her statements, Dallas had seemed to stop noticing the people walking past, to really focus into what Danni was saying, noticing that it was different from what he usually nodded his head and grinned about. "You're a bad girl," he said. "You know that, right? Not so obvious, I dig that."

Danni glanced over at Kizzy who was flirting with some guys by the fence. If Danni could just take one step, maybe she'd be able to make a mad dash away from the vibe that she was feeling, a desire that she wasn't sure if she could handle. If his bedroom, heavy eyes surveyed her body one more time, she wasn't sure how she was going to react. Dallas Laylock was producing bursts of sensations in Danni's chest, and now she couldn't get rid of the goofy grin on her face. She tried to avoid eye contact with him, but *that's* when she caught that look in his eyes, that might-not-getcha-now . . .

He didn't say a word, and seemed comfortable with the silence. There was the sound of a piece of paper ruffling as he pulled it from his pocket. He wrote something down on the back of a receipt and slipped to Danni. His autograph. *To Danni, with the smile. D. Laylock*, and cell phone digits were there as well.

It took a week of Kizzy's girl-if-you-don't-call-that-man-you-stupid-wench speeches for Danni to get up the nerve to call. When she finally did, she got his voice mail. He called her back the day after that. And then it was on, she was the mouse, he the cat. And for two years, Danni had been trapped.

And now Dallas was back, that same look on his face.

But please. The whole glitz thing, the whole superstar thing, the whole he's-a-millionaire-and-is-so-fly thing? No thanks. This was a new day, a more mature, a very much improved state of mind for Danni. From the jump-start of her life, she had been abandoned, left in a plastic basket on the porch of the foster home where she grew up, but *still* she grew up with a smile on her face. Now she would just have to fight like hell if she had to, to find that same peace. Nobody was ever going to leave her again. Ever.

"Why the tight fists." He touched her hand. "Why so tense? Sittin' over there lookin' you're ready to punch me or something."

There were no body bags, no bloodshed, none of the stuff on CNN, but this was Danni's war. Her heart was at stake. From now on she would be more vigilant, a soldier for herself.

He said, "So what's up with lunch?"

"I have lunch every day," she said. "Been having lunch every day for the last two months as a matter of fact."

"Here you go."

"It was nice that we happened to run into each other, okay?"

"I made you laugh though, didn't I?"

"And?"

"A woman laughing is a woman conquered," he said. "Check it out, right from my man Napoleon."

Danni remembered how Dallas was always reading some book, always quoting somebody, always wanting to debate something. If she humored him, asked him what he'd just read up on Napoleon, Dallas would get a pound of gratification in his eyes as he prepared to give her a history lesson, D.L. style.

"My man Napoleon," he began. "Now that muh-fucka right there—"

"Look. Before you even start," Danni said, "I know you just love reading up on all these supposedly great men in history, Dallas, but I don't really care about Napoleon or anybody else you care to quote. A great man is an honest one regardless of whether or not you can read a book about him."

"Let's just get away for a minute. Take a trip. So we can talk. Wherever you wanna go."

"Dallas, *please*," was Danni's reply.

Damn some trip to Tahiti or Monte Carlo, Danni was ready for Dallas to bring things up a tax bracket, for him to start giving her the kind of stuff that his by-invitation-only Centurion American Express couldn't buy, things she'd never had. Like loyalty. Like stability. And how about a first-class trip through his soul, for him to just at least *try* to be as insatiable for her spirit as he was for her body. Look at him, sex still in his eyes. Maybe breaking up *had* been a good thing.

She reached for the handle. "You take care, all right?"

Dallas did know some things about Danni, all of what he'd said had been true. But, surprise, surprise, the whole time they'd been sitting in his truck, Danni hadn't whined about needing him, about missing him. She hadn't bolted at the opportunity to have a chance again, to go with him on some spontaneous trip. Danni opened the door and got out. Bet he didn't know that she was capable of *that*.

• • •

"So, what else did he say?" Kizzy had turned the music off on the drive home. "Looked like a phat truck, from what I could see, the way he was peeling out of the parking lot all fast like that."

Danni found the groove of the headrest and relaxed her neck. She closed her eyes and sighed. "Just like I told you. That was it. Lunch, dinner, let's go on a trip. Same ole, same ole. Wanting to know if I'm seeing anybody."

"What'd you say? 'Naw fool I'm waitin' around on you to get your act together.'"

"Never the-I'm-lost-without-you role for me. Please." Danni sighed as they pulled up in front of her building. "Really, to be honest, all I wanna do is go upstairs, paint, and be happy. Dallas can go on about his business for all I care."

Kizzy put the car in park. "You might meet a new man tonight. You still haven't told me what you're gonna wear."

Danni unsnapped the barrette from her hair, and let her ponytail fall. "I'm tired of all this." She took a piece of her hair and bent the end up to frown at it. "It's too hot for all this extra hair."

"So," Kizzy suggested. "Wear it up in a bun. What time should we get there tonight?"

"I don't know, Kiz." Danni pushed her shades up the bridge of her nose until they were more snug against her face. "Call me later."

"You *are* still going tonight, right?"

"Call me," Danni said again as she closed the door.

. . .

The inside of Danni's pad felt stuffy, too still, and it shocked her. She felt weary all of a sudden, overwhelmingly so, didn't feel like taking a shower, didn't even bother getting out of her workout clothes. She pulled back the sheers, let the sun pour a warm orange haze over her white living-room furniture, and opened the windows.

The room filled with noises of downtown traffic, but Bumpy's salsa music, coming from the loft above her, was even louder.

Danni stretched out on the couch, sticking and skidding on the leather until she settled into a comfortable position. The breeze relaxed the room, and she snatched the remote.

Any other time, she would have snapped her fingers to the beat, but right now she didn't want a reason to move, didn't want to think about anything, didn't even want to *look* at her canvas. She had to push the volume all the way up to twenty just to drown out Celia Cruz.

Reports on CNN were too depressing.

On some dating show, a busty woman who knew nothing more about her rendezvous partner than his name and the fact that his stomach was so ripped that it could've sliced paper, was willing to put her mouth on any part of his body just to be chosen? Puh-leez.

Several movies, already in progress.

That comedian Sommore was on Comic View. A guaranteed laugh for sure, so Danni put the remote down. The jokes came, were relentlessly funny as expected, but Danni couldn't laugh.

Deciding to just try and enjoy Bumpy's muffled music, Danni turned off the tube. Maybe if she just let go, she could lose herself in the rhythm, shake some of the funk.

She imagined Bumpy, a middle-aged woman, her hair rolled onto those big green rollers, covered by a purple silk scarf, probably standing in the middle of her living room, stabbing the area rug with her signature silver stilettos. Her right hand across her stomach, her left one holding a cigarette above her head, probably doing a serious salsa, alone.

Danni pictured Bumpy's eyes, oval, brown, and pensive, and she thought about the Halloween-orange lipstick Bumpy usually wore. Danni could've, if she'd felt like it, created a portrait from memory alone, could've given it to Bumpy for Christmas.

But Danni just lay there.

And that song kept playing. Over and over and over.

Maybe Bumpy was lying across her couch, too, solemn, thinking about her deceased husband, her companion of twenty-two years. Perhaps that had been their song? In that case, the painting would need to be dark and moody. Danni would have to cast extra shadows, intensify Bumpy's eyes, change the lipstick to brown.

Still, Danni did not get up.

Maybe Bumpy had a new lover? Maybe right now he was holding her. Maybe he was a handsome man she'd met at the market. Maybe he had a thick mustache and passion in his eyes. Maybe he'd taken one look at Bumpy, a beautiful but lonely woman, and knew just what to do. Maybe he'd walked over and introduced himself in a polite and respectful way, proving that he recognized her for the lady she was. Maybe Bumpy was having him over for dinner right now, and that song was playing over dessert. Perhaps they were dancing.

But Danni didn't get up, didn't make one solitary effort to transpose any of those reflections onto the canvas, now a motion picture of images playing out in her mind. Once upon a time, before Danni even knew who Dallas Laylock was, she would have been unable to rest until she'd finished. But she didn't even get up, didn't even start.

Those stones were just some silly project that she'd thought about beginning. Who was she kidding? She hadn't been a dedicated artist in over two years. Oh sure, she'd dipped and pecked while Dallas was on the road sometimes, when she wasn't working overtime, hanging out with Kizzy, whenever she'd actually had some time on her hands, but that had been rare.

It felt similar to running into a friend you hadn't seen in years, someone with whom you were once inseparable. You're so happy to see them at first, can't swap stories and exchange thoughts fast enough, but then . . . too much time has passed. Maybe all you have is the memories, the way things used to be.

For the last few weeks Danni's strokes had been so determined to rekindle what she knew had been lying dormant for too long, but maybe it was pointless. Maybe she and her first love, the only true friend besides Kiz that she had while growing up, had grown apart.

Whatever the case, those stones and that paint would be there tomorrow if Danni felt up to giving it another go. For now she was shoulder-deep back in a funk again. She needed to rest. And that's what she did.

• • •

It was almost six o'clock and downtown was getting quiet, the calm before the nightlife. Danni had just a few hours before things would be loud and indignant, before the clubs started jumping and she'd have to close her windows. She wanted to have a nice, calm dinner beforehand, and had just finished chopping broccoli when the phone rang.

"Hey," she answered.

Kizzy's voice was as hyped as ever. "Wuz up, wuz up, wuz up? What's hap-nin', fly?"

"Chillin'," Danni held the phone slightly away from her ear. "You sound happy."

Kizzy smacked her lips. "*Chillin?* Girrrrl . . ."

"That's right."

"Umm-hmm. Well, I say we need to do appetizers at Sweet Georgia Brown before we make our entrance at the party."

Danni looked at the little hills of chopped carrots, peas, diced onions, rice, sprouts, and raw chicken laid out in front of her, the hot oil waiting in the wok. "Sorry," she said. "I've already started cooking."

"Girl, come on. It'll be fun. Meet me there in twenty minutes?"

"I'm really not up to it."

"Oh, girl, come on." Kizzy was even more excited now. "You *have* to come with me."

"I don't know if I feel up to it, Kiz. Plus, I've got work do."

"What? Some painting, I guess?"

"Uh, artist. Hello. Remember?"

"I know, but . . ."

"There are no buts." Danni slammed her knife down through another onion. "That is what I do."

A pause. "But you're coming with me to the party at least, right?"

"I'm sorry, Kiz."

"Girl, now you *know* it's gonna be wall-to-wall geniuses at that party, just parlaying, spending ends like what. You never know who might be there . . ."

Exactly.

"Thanks," Danni said. "I'm cool."

"Come on, Dan."

"I'm sorry . . . Don't be mad at me, all right?"

"Well, I'm not trippin'. It's not that serious. I just want you to get out tonight. Are you sure? Positive. Really, really, really, absolutely—"

"Two hundred percent, Kiz. *Really.*"

"And you'll call me, hit me up if you change your mind? Because you know I'm still gonna kick it. You know me. I'm trying to see who I can see, and who I can let see me."

"And you're gonna look fly, Kiz. Fabulous. I hope you meet your prince."

"Yeah, but you know, it won't be the same without my partner in flyness."

"I'll call if I change my mind."

"Promise?"

"Promise."

Kizzy waited, hope still lingering in the air. "Call me later, regardless though. Okay?"

"I will," she replied.

Danni hung up the phone, tossed the strips of chicken in the wok, and stared down at the oil, listening to every sizzle and watching every pop.

She looked down at the knife she was holding, and eyed the tresses hanging down over her shoulder. She sat the blade down on the stove, reached for the drawer at the end of the counter, and snatched up the scissors.

Now sitting on the edge of the bathroom sink, with one swoop of her thumb, Danni parted her hair straight across the back. She lifted the upper half up, what was naturally hers, and twisted it, clipping it all on top of her head.

She positioned herself so that if she cut her eye just right she could get a clear view, and she eyed the lump, the track of hair skillfully sewn onto a very thin horizontal braid of her own hair. She took a deep breath.

She could have, if she had the patience and felt like trying, found the tiny hints of thread and snipped them out bit by bit, letting the weave fall, leaving hers intact. She could have waited, called up her beautician, and let *her* cut out the tracks, but Danni probably wouldn't have been able to get an appointment until next week.

Fully aware that she was going to damage her own hair, Danni still put the scissors to her scalp and cut, intentionally severing her own skinny braid and all. Before that track had even hit the sink, Danni was in search of the next one.

After she was finished, it was difficult at first, to lift her face to the mirror. She stared down at the pile of fake hair lying in the sink, but surprisingly felt no regret, felt accomplished even. Her head felt much lighter, and Danni felt bare. She wondered if she was going to look peculiar.

She did not.

Her actual hair grazed just a little past her shoulders, and though it looked much finer than it had in years, it was surprisingly refreshing to see it. Once it was flat-ironed, Danni was sure it would actually look kinda good. Better than good.

She examined her face, up close and focused. When had this become not good enough? Two years ago Danni had let Kizzy talk her into this mess, and a month after that was when Danni had met Dallas. So maybe Kiz had been right, that a little more hair would add a lot more appeal. But please. It was time for the mirror to truly reflect who Danni used to be, who she truly always was.

She should've known better than to think that something so magical, so wonderful as being loved by, wanted by, and maybe even *married to* a man as incredible as Dallas Laylock would happen to a girl like her.

Maybe for some people it's cool to dream, awesome to believe, amazing when those dreams come true. But that was never gonna be the case for Danni. Never had been. All she ever wanted, her whole life growing up, was to paint, to travel the world creating, and to someday marry a man she loved. She should have known better. Her own parents had cast her aside. Why wouldn't her passion? Why wouldn't he?

Back in the kitchen, after finishing the preparation of her stir-fry, Danni unplugged the landline and turned the power off on her cell phone. She sat down at the dining-room table and crossed one leg over the other. If she was meant to be alone then she would just eat dinner unaccompanied, by herself, with herself, with nobody else. And she would enjoy it.

On Monday it would be back to work, back to the grind, the last-minute tasks before the big opening that week, and Danni might as well enjoy this quiet time while she could. On Monday she would put on her makeup, her rosy-cheeked and glossy-lipped mask of joy, and go to work. And, like always, if anyone asked her how she was doing, no matter if she still felt this heaviness in her chest, Danni would reply with the words *fine thanks, and you.*

Her knuckles touched the glass of the dining-room table.

Tap. Tap. Tap. In war, that's what a soldier hears, the sound of a drum beating, each thump more thunderous, pounding more courage into their souls. All her life, no matter how uncertain she'd ever felt, Danni, too, had had to keep her head lifted, to march on.

It wasn't all the way true, what Napoleon said. In the first place Danni was definitely not a woman interested in being *conquered*. And on the contrary, a woman laughing, *truly* expressing how she's been affected by something humorous, is either a happy soul or, as in Danni's case, a woman who knows what she's got to do to keep from crying.

two

china by way of france

Even though it was Monday evening, random remarks were still bouncing around the conference room like a chaotic game of Ping-Pong. Danni's eyes were heavy, the only part of her still able to follow her coworker's voices. She ran her hand over her hair, pulled back into a neat bun, and leaned over to Garvey, their resident graphic designer, who was doodling a Marvel-looking cartoon character. She asked him for the time.

"Time for a Newport," he whispered back, his breath already thick with after-smoke. And was that a hint of liquor she smelled? Garvey slid out his pocket watch. "Ten 'til eight," he informed her.

The primary purpose of ReveNations was *supposed* to be

providing downtown Detroit with a medium for very talented but emerging young artists to present their innovative and never-before-exhibited work. The constant hitch, of course, was alluring the general public. That's where the publicist came in. Or had, anyhow.

Just last month, their publicist had quit because, well, with funding steadily decreasing over the last six months, she had feared capsizing with the ship. And, as she was the publicist's still-standing assistant, it was no wonder everyone had their eyebrows raised at Danni. It wasn't like she had a master's degree, a four-year even, and could just take the wheel. All she really knew for sure were the basics. More press more hype, more hype more people, more people more funding, more funding better job security. She could write press releases, work the Rolodex, and make contacts when necessary, but she'd be the first to admit that she had plenty to learn. Still, ReveNations was Danni's ark, her only financial means of staying afloat without Dallas, and she would do whatever it took and then some, for that place.

She glanced across the table at N'Drea, their warden. Actually, she was the chief proprietor and curator. A statuesque woman, she wore her natural cut very close. N'Drea was the type of woman who'd come over for a visit and notice the crumbs on your counter, dusting them off with a quick brush of her hand as she did.

It was *Danni's* job to ensure that their artists got the media attention their opening deserved, but right now N'Drea, dressed in her customary I'm-most-important attire, was toy-ing with her ancient-artifact-looking earring, and asking *the entire room* if anyone had any suggestions for media outreach.

Garvey was sitting next to Danni, an obligatory alert look on his face, but now he actually did perk up a bit to watch Danni on the sly. Having Garvey around reminded Danni of what it would be like to work with a fellow trapeze artist, someone always on the other side, watching you carefully, just in case they needed to step in and help. He tapped Danni's leg, a be-cool reminder.

Danni gave him a real quick I'm-okay look, and then she began massaging her own neck with the tips of her oval-filed fingernails. She tilted her head until she heard that popping noise, then she tilted it the other way until it made that sound again. Her metal mug had REVENATIONS written in silver lettering across the front, and she took that last hit of caffeine before clearing her throat. "Uh, I've already handled the press releases, N'Drea," Danni reminded her.

N'Drea rumbled through all of the paperwork in front of her and glanced over what looked like a résumé. "Well, then I trust that the press is aware that our guest artist hails from Howard University with a bachelor's in art, minor in psychology. An advanced degree from CalArts . . ."

Danni tuned out N'Drea's droning on and on with the brotha's credentials. Yes, he was coming equipped with all of these fancy degrees, but what had he learned, how did he *feel* about art? Wasn't that what ReveNations was supposed to represent? The *love* of art? Leave it to N'Drea to nevermind all of that. "Yes," Danni assured her. "All of that was included in the releases, N'Drea. Trust me. You approved them weeks ago."

For a brief moment, Danni wondered what anyone would be able to say about *her* if ever she achieved her goal, if ever it was her opening that some gallery was prepping for. All she had was an associate's in fine arts from Wayne State University, and a stack of repayment coupons from student loans as a monthly reminder. She should've let Dallas pay them off when he'd offered.

"Oh." N'Drea winked. "Very good, Danni. *Very* good."

Danni leaned in, whispered to Garvey, "Any more jelly doughnuts left?"

He tried hard to hold in his laughter, but it came out via a snort.

N'Drea slipped on her reading glasses and looked out over the top. "Uh, Mr. Douglass?"

Garvey sat up and gave his suspenders a tug. "Yes?"

N'Drea pursed her lips. "You had a comment? A question or concern? Something to contribute to this discussion?"

"No, ma'am."

N'Drea turned stiffly, and smiled at Danni. "Ms. Blair? Anything?"

"Uh, no," Danni put on a spirited face. "None from me."

"Good, then."

Danni reached for the doughnut box, and once she saw that it was empty, she flipped the lid closed and sighed. Damn, she was hungry.

N'Drea looked around the room at the seven team members present, and said, "Perhaps that's all?"

Whew. Danni needed some fresh air, some ice water, and a

cup of coffee. Maybe then she would be fully awake. There was an abundance of things that still needed to be accomplished before she went home for the evening.

Garvey touched Danni's shoulder. "Goin' for that Newport." He got up and left.

But N'Drea didn't leave the room when the others did. She made her way around to Danni's side of the table.

"Ms. Blair," she said. "If you would. May I speak with you, please?"

"Oh, sure," Danni replied.

The sounds of the head-woman-in-charge's thick heels warned Danni of her proximity, that she was standing directly behind her. N'Drea's cologne was a very thick, very overbearing musk, one that only someone who'd changed her name to a more-fitting-for-an-owner-of-an-art-gallery-sounding one, dropping her surname, would wear. She sat down in Garvey's seat and asked Danni, "How are you?"

"Just fine, thanks," Danni looked over and said. "And yourself?"

"Good." N'Drea's face faded into a concerned look. "I know, with the breakup—"

"Oh." Danni stopped her. "Things happen, you know. Next chapter. It's been two months. I'm just focused on moving on."

N'Drea looked like she found that hard to believe, but regardless, she said, "What an admirable attitude. I know you two were very—"

"N'Drea," Danni interrupted. "Please. Let me spare you the speech. I'm okay."

"Just making sure you haven't been too, you know, overwhelmed, with the project. Letting go is difficult. And relationships *can* affect us."

"Everything is coming along well," Danni assured her. "I spoke with Roman Bilal on Friday and plan to touch base with him tomorrow afternoon."

"Good," N'Drea looked pleased.

"And, definitely," Danni said. "For sure. Whatever it takes to make this opening successful . . ."

"Utilize the team. With so much to accomplish, the last thing you need is to spend unnecessary time stuck in a muddle of rhetoric, making phone calls, et cetera."

"It's no problem." Danni smiled. "Whatever it takes."

"I know I can count on you," N'Drea offered. "You've always had such a terrific can-do attitude. I appreciate that about you."

"Well, thank you," Danni answered merrily.

"*That* outlook," N'Drea sounded like she was giving an oration, "is so infectious, and so vital to a team's productivity."

And keeping with the tradition of her dramatic I've-got-places-to-go-and-people-to-call style, N'Drea left the room without another word. For now.

. . .

A while later, after her second glass of ice water, Danni was working in the main gallery, enjoying its spacious solitude. She stepped back, her eyes exploring twelve hundred square feet of absolute whiteness. All walls, the ceiling, and the freshly waxed limestone floor were so flawless.

Tomorrow evening, the room was going to swell with on-lookers and Danni was considering exactly where the steel easel should go. As she hugged it, she scowled at the likelihood that the artist was probably sitting at home at that very moment, taking it all for granted.

Since she'd begun working at ReveNations, Danni had encountered more than enough artists who possessed an abundance of talent but lacked humility, had a way of talking *at* people, her especially, and being off-putting to the public. Danni exhaled. And here she was setting the stage for yet another spectacular ego exhibition.

Would this artist be like Edgar, the five-foot sculptor from New Jersey who whispered when he spoke? Who'd insisted that all patrons enter the gallery in silence, their shoes left at the door so as not to make any noise while they walked in, and they weren't to say a word, not one single solitary word, while they gazed at his sculpture of a sleeping baby?

Or the performance artist, Victim she called herself, who used her own naked body as a feminist exhibit, blue felt-tip marker pointing to various parts on her nut-brown body. An arrow on her cheek pointing to her mouth and the words *tongue = strongest muscle*, and an arrow going from her navel to somewhere in her thick pubic hair, with the word *LIFE* written in all capital letters at the top. Only three people attended.

Or maybe, hopefully, he would be more like Tobi Cauley, another woman, statuesque but *only* in spirit. Her quilting exhibit was, by far, the most successful that Danni had had the pleasure of helping to promote. And Tobi, so giving, so kind, had spoken with Danni extensively afterward. "Go," she'd told her when Danni shared her own artistic dreams. "Go forth and release."

The door into that wing of the gallery was glass, so a whisper of air let Danni know that she now had company. N'Drea's voice shoved her right out of the memories, out of her private peace and quiet.

"Oh, Ms. Blair," she said, her voice too loud in the silence. "I was hoping to find you in here."

Danni smiled. "Well, here I am."

"Nervous?"

Danni turned to face her. "Not really. Not at all, actually. I used to give speeches in high school debate all the time. Should I be?"

"Good for you." She winked. "I was, the week of my first speech, a basket case. Oh, but that was many, many years ago. It's admirable that you're not."

N'Drea hummed an uninspired note, stared at the ceiling, the walls, the floor. She did this as if she was seeing it all for the first time, as if she herself had not dictated the placement of every tiny speck of winter-white paint.

Danni asked, "Is everything okay?"

N'Drea's eyes darted everywhere except in Danni's direction. When she couldn't avoid looking at her any longer, she took a very theatrical breath. This made Danni give her a look, a reminder that she knew her real name was Andrenita Jones.

Responding to the don't-go-there repellent aimed at her, N'Drea let out a hearty laugh and toned it down a notch.

"Danni, we're all just so excited to hear what you've prepared, me especially."

Danni gripped the easel, turned back to face the room, to focus on deciding, and explained as she dragged it, "It's always like looking out into the universe, you know? Like trying to figure out where to place the earth."

"Need any help?"

"Nope," Danni replied. "I think I can handle it. What's this, my tenth, twelfth opening?"

And then N'Drea was quiet again. "I appreciate you picking up responsibilities during the void, volunteering to give the speech, being such a go-getter. That's what *real* team members do."

An unsure laugh escaped from Danni's mouth. Why did N'Drea keep going on and on about this? "I uh, I guess, you know, having worked on so many openings . . . Not like this is my first, you know. I know since Rashida quit things have been a little less organized, but I feel real good about the opening."

"Yes indeed." N'Drea took a long blink. "That's one of the best ways to learn, just dive in and be hands-on. Certainly. I trust that Rashida trained you well. You look tired. Everything okay?"

"Oh." Danni rolled her eyes a little. "I'm fine. I feel great." She left out the part that it was now after nine o'clock at night, that she'd been there since eight A.M.

"Oh, well, good. And, uh . . ."

"Yes?" Danni's laugh was apprehensive.

"Just wondering if you'll be able to join us on Thursday evening?"

Danni tried to recall where all of her coworkers were going for their post-opening evening of bonding; where they would all probably lock arms like the Rockettes to stroll through Greektown singing that Sister Sledge song about family. Danni wasn't interested, didn't really care about wherever it was that they had peeked into her office last week and asked her to join. Besides, she'd probably be too tired from all the "team" work that she had yet to do.

Still tonight, Danni had the guest list to go over again. Again, she had to make sure that every artist, local celebrity, and distinguished person that had confirmed his or her intent to attend the reception was on the list, plus one, for tomorrow night.

She had to ensure that things were in line for the reception.

Even if she wanted to, which she did not, Danni probably would be too tired from the week to go catch a—*oh yeah*—that's where they were going, to catch a flick.

Tonight Danni needed to rehearse her brief welcome—the verbal tribute she had been assigned months ago to give on behalf of the artist. Who was she kidding? She still had to write the damn thing.

She was cautious not to scrape the floor as she toted the easel to the center of the room. She asked, "What movie are you guys going to go see?"

"Garvey was telling us about a student-produced documentary. Well, I guess they were students when they started making it. The buzz is Oscar nomination. We'll probably have drinks beforehand."

Danni stood the easel upright, straightened out its legs before she stepped back again. "Supposed to be that good, huh? Oscar nomination? Wow. That's impressive."

"Indeed. That is the buzz."

Danni wished then that a few minutes ago she had told N'Drea that she did have the jitters, then maybe she would have realized that Danni really didn't care to hear about some documentary right now. But, in an effort to be polite, Danni said, "Sounds like fun."

"So, you'll join us?"

"Oh, N'Drea . . . I'm so sorry. I have plans," Danni lied.

The tone in her voice shifted a bit. "Danni," N'Drea said. "We're not that bad."

Danni's eyes rippled in confusion. "*Huh?* What do you mean?"

"Your coworkers. Myself. Danni, let's be real. No one is any busier than I am, okay? As chief executive of this entire establishment I have to tie all the loose ends. Me. I'm the first to get here and the last to go home. Every single day. Plus I've got three kids. And a spouse who, let me tell you, doesn't hold these events in the same regard as I. *All* of us are busy."

"Well, I don't mean it like that," Danni said. "Whatever it takes for the opening."

N'Drea continued. "Not a single word has changed in the mission statement. We all respect the need for camaraderie among our team."

"Oh, of course," Danni agreed.

"My MBA," N'Drea said, "took me to a six-figure job, right

out of graduate school, Danni, yet I was destitute for happiness. For eleven years. And I swore that if I ever realized my dream, whenever I owned my own, ran my own, foremost, above any profit, I would insist on maintaining a team atmosphere."

Danni accidentally hit her hand on the side of the easel as her arm swung upward to scratch her forehead. It hadn't been itching. Danni would be miserable for eleven years, too, if it took her *that* long to save up enough to do what she really wanted to do, if she was still working *here* eleven years from now, still not back in touch with her art or at least something that made her feel more validated. She swallowed, hoped that she had done so unnoticeably, and replied, "It's nothing personal, N'Drea."

N'Drea continued, "Jacob Jr. has the chicken pox, and Dinah keeps trying to get in the room with him, wants to play doctor with her toy kit. We all have lives and situations, Danni, people who need us outside of the team. Jonathan, Isyss, most of your superiors even have second jobs to worry about. Garvey's in the final stretch to his master's. Johnetta's just beginning."

Danni wondered why, if things were that busy and hectic, any of them were silly enough to want to sit up in a movie theater eating popcorn this weekend. Shouldn't they be studying?

"Look," Danni said. "I'll tell you what, I'll join you guys for a drink, how's that?"

N'Drea took a big long breath. "Good enough." She winked her signature phony wink. And then she flipped back to the real issue. "We're all anticipating your speech. With so many key investors confirmed to attend, we could really spark some financial interest in our vision, providing all goes well."

N'Drea shook her head. "Because I'll be blunt. Nine eleven or no nine eleven, we're still feeling the sting from a pretty brutal economic slap. We can't lose what funding we still have, and we simply *must* increase contributions."

Danni wanted to laugh. She seriously wanted to crack up laughing like a hyena. The dim economy wasn't the only reason for those constant dollar signs in N'Drea's eyes. Please. She also had that Auburn Hills mortgage, her children's Montessori education to pay for.

"And you know." N'Drea cupped her chin in her hand. "And it's probably not a *huge* deal, but if you have any spare time, perhaps you could assist Isyss with the finishing touches on Thursday's ads?"

"Sure thing," Danni agreed.

"I really want things to go exceptionally well for the VIP reception tomorrow, and for the opening this weekend."

"We didn't come this far to have things flop," Danni assured her.

Then N'Drea offered another of her condescending winks. "Some people measure, take an actual tape measurer and everything, in order to mark the exact center of the room. And place the easel there."

"Thanks." Danni stretched the easel's legs out again, and left it close to the wall, far away from the center of the room.

N'Drea chuckled. "Or not. That could work."

"I'll just leave it be," Danni said. "You know how artists can be. When they get here they always have their say."

"Things can always be moved."

"Right," Danni replied.

A moment later, N'Drea added, "Oh. And then there's this issue with the wine."

"Okay." Danni made a mental note to also cover the administrative assistant's duties while trying to complete her own within the teeny amount of time she had left before tomorrow night.

And away those heels clicked. Once again, the air whispered. Only the scent of N'Drea's perfume lingered.

• • •

Garvey didn't bother to knock, just popped right into Danni's office. By now he had pulled his dreadlocks back into a fat ponytail, and he slapped a folded newspaper onto her desk, pulled up a chair, and yawned.

"Your boy made the paper again," he said.

Danni ignored him, focusing instead on the speech that she had started writing. She asked him, "Have I ever told you how much I adore you?"

"Not yet today. I'm waiting."

But Danni's thoughts were elsewhere, she wasn't as sharp with her quips today.

It is my distinct pleasure to introduce to you none other than one of our great city's most esteemed up-and-coming artistic heroes . . .

Danni shuddered at the thought of having to write this by tomorrow. Why had she done this to herself?

Garvey's voice boomed in. "If I were you, I'd slap N'Drea. Corner her and just bang her one real hard, right in the mouth, like you're the mother and she's your little smart-mouthed heathen. Like my mama used to do us."

"Please." A laugh slipped out of Danni's mouth. "And do what, go work at Burger King?"

He lowered his voice. "You know she's been complaining about you not coming with us on the past several bond nights. Better watch it."

"Really?"

"Uh-hum. You know how she is, team this and team that."

"Please."

He laughed.

The more she thought about it, the more Danni had to vent. She said, "All this work to accomplish, and as much extra as I'm always more than willing to do, and she's got time to worry about how I spend my evenings?"

"I know."

"I deserve more digits on my salary, all of this overtime I've been putting in."

"You sure do."

"But I never ask for a raise. I may as well work straight through 'til tomorrow."

"Like you *always* do."

"Please."

"I know that's right."

"And just a few minutes ago," Danni said, "she's all acting like I'm so important to the team."

"But, you know now, you ain't heard none of this from me."

"Not a word," Danni pledged. "How'd your blind date go last night?"

"Repulsive. I had to fake a stomachache to get out of coffee after dinner. Had nightmares. Had to have a drink on my way to work and everything."

"You're so terrible," Danni laughed.

"No," he said. "What's terrible is that it was only our first date, but already I can tell you that she almost did time for trying to set her ex-husband's ding-a-ling on fire."

"Ooh. TMI, my brotha."

"My *sista,*" he said. "You think *that's* too much information? You should've heard what she told me about her childhood."

"I don't even wanna know."

"Then she started drillin' *me,* made me feel like I was back in boot camp. Had to bust out of there just like I did the army."

"Are you serious?"

"Do you rent or own? Any kids? Name, address, and phone number of your last three girlfriends? And listen, we hadn't even ordered appetizers yet."

"You have to be exaggerating."

"And she was cute too. Thick. The pimp in me took one look at those watermelon thighs, big juicy pumpkin booty, and I wanted to play it like I cared. Just long enough so I could get me some of that. Had to cancel that plan though, real quick.

Probably would've ended up in some kind of playa protection program, would've had to relocate and all that."

"Yeah." Danni pulled open her bottom drawer and retrieved a manila folder. "Well, you just remember this. That woman was not born that way. *Life* did that to her. Foul-ass men did that to her."

He whispered, "So, what's up with you and Laylock?"

"And you bring him up because . . . ?"

"You know." He brushed nothing off his shoulder. "The chip and all."

"Well, back to the subject worth talking about, *you* need to check your attitude about women. And I *don't* have a chip on my shoulder, damn it."

"Shoot, when I finally do get me a fine woman to break off them panties, it's over for the game, 'cause I'm tryin' to keep hittin' it like a LP on skip. Know what I'm sayin'?"

Then he started in on the whole while-they-were-crying-about-wanting-one-women-didn't-know-how-to-recognize-a-good-man-sitting-right-in-front-of-them.

If Danni had cared enough, she'd have probably broken the news to him, would have told him that the real reason he didn't get far with women was because he talked too damn much. And that confidence was one thing, but arrogance was fatal. And that getting a woman to break off her panties shouldn't be his main concern, that getting to know her mind should be. Another reason she didn't discuss this topic further with Garvey, however, was because she'd have never gotten him out of her office if she had. Thank goodness her phone buzzed.

She hit the intercom. "Yes?"

"Kizzy, on line one."

"Uh, take a message please," Danni replied. "Tell her I'm still tied up, that I'll call her back a little later."

The phone placed back on the receiver, Danni turned around and asked Garvey, "So, what's up?"

"Not much. Want a hot cup or something?"

"No." Danni sighed. She picked up the manila folder and pretended like the papers inside were of dire importance. She flipped through them, one by one, and the words were blurred and incomprehensible. Too much work. Hardly enough time. If Garvey would just leave her alone she'd have silence again, could think more clearly.

"Thanks, though," she added.

Garvey just sat there. A few moments later, he finally leaned in, tried to get a glimpse of her computer screen, but Danni had learned her lesson a long time ago, had strategically placed the monitor so that his nosy ass couldn't see.

He asked her, "What is it, your speech?"

"It is."

"How's it going?"

The screen looked so much larger than it ever had, but she still replied, "Great."

"Wanna run it by me?" he asked.

"Maybe later." But at least he'd offered. "Thanks," she said.

"No problem."

"You're not busy the rest of the night, are you?"

He gave her a look.

Of course he was. Everyone was always busy whenever *Danni* needed a favor.

He said, "I've really got some reading to do for class."

Danni sighed at the screen. Eff it. She could just do the best she could. "Don't worry about it," she told him.

"I'm sorry. If I could stay, you know I would. I owe you a few."

"Indebted for life." Danni gave him one of N'Drea's phony winks. "And don't you forget it."

He laughed. "Listen," he said. "Also, real quick, before I go, can you go over Thursday and Friday's ads before Isyss sends them out?" He plopped a black floppy on her desk.

"I know."

"And one more—"

"No," she interrupted. "All messengers of any additional work for Danni must leave. Immediately. Good-bye." She laughed.

"Seriously," he said. "Stop playin'. We need to know if we had the wine chilled or room temperature last month."

"Am I the only one who was *here* last month?"

"Never mind. Send me an e-mail if you remember, so I can forward it on. We'll need to know by tomorrow morning."

Whoops. Danni needed to check her e-mail. She pulled the Outlook box up on her screen. Seven new messages.

He continued, "And Isyss can't find the number to confirm the valet attendants."

"Tell her to talk to Johnetta, will you? She's in charge of it. Still. Like always." That would buy Danni some time to look up the information before Johnetta eventually popped her head in Danni's office and asked the same thing.

Garvey stood up, clicked his heels, and saluted her. "Your wish, my command." And he left.

Danni's intercom buzzed again.

"Yes?"

"Ms. Blair." The intern smiled through the phone again. "Just reminding you of the ten o'clock tomorrow morning. I'm getting ready to leave."

Danni could have thrown the phone. "Thanks," she said. "See you in the morning."

• • •

Danni really didn't feel like this shit tonight.

It was after midnight, and she was five minutes shy of home, when she noticed an older model Chevy Impala trailing close behind her.

Two blocks away, she knew she was being followed.

Now that she was one block away, Danni reached into her back seat and felt around for her Louisville Slugger.

It was downtown on a weeknight, so the streets were fairly quiet, just Danni and whoever the hell this was.

The intimidating and determined bright headlights were immediately behind her as she slowed down on her street.

Her insistent shadow did the same.

If this turned out to be some skirt-chasing pervert, trying to grab hold of her wraparound, Danni was going to make sure he regretted it when he regained consciousness. She settled into a parking space on the street, and gripped her weapon. Whoever he was had picked the wrong day to be stupid. She was overworked, tired, and hungry.

Out of the corner of her eye, she could see the tinted windows crawling up beside her. If this jerk turned out to be a psychopath, the last thing she wanted to do was look like a victim. She wasn't in the best physical shape she'd ever been in her life, but she would just have to work with what she had.

She yanked the keys from her ignition, tightened her grip on the baseball bat, and stepped out. Her right hand was heavy at her waist and ready to swing if necessary, and even though the black windows prohibited her from seeing a face, Danni picked up the pace of her stride. Her adrenaline was raged.

A head-nodding beat became more audible as the window rolled down.

Danni exhaled.

He leaned over and nodded up. "What up?" He was grinning. As if his unexpected visit was normal, or even acceptable.

Relieved, Danni shook her head and sighed. Irritated, she glared. "You follow me for blocks, pull up beside me, trying to scare somebody, *and* it's late on top of that! Do you *really* wanna know what's up?" She showed him her bat.

Dallas bit his bottom lip in an effort not to laugh. "Like you know what to do with that. I got my mitt in the trunk. What up?" He opened his door and got out, leaving the car right in the middle of the street with the ignition running.

"And whose car is that?"

"Mine. Just a toy. When I wanna be low-key."

She wanted to shove him as much as she wanted to give him a hug for not being some mad rapist or murderer or something. "What are you doing here?"

He gave her thigh a pinch. "What up?"

She leaned her bat against a tree. "Are you gonna answer my question?"

"I followed you," he said.

"No shit," she replied.

His eyes widened. His smile grew. "My bad. I really scared you?"

She gave him a what-do-you-think look.

He said, "Kinda late for you to be just getting home."

"I'm a grown woman," she said. "And what? You're out—*late.*"

"I just left a set though."

"Good for you. Get your dance on?"

"Not really. Just a few drinks. Rock's birthday. What'd you do, kick it wit' your new man tonight?"

"And then what? Left from getting your drink on and decided, hey, I've got an idea, I'll go scare the pants off of Danni tonight?"

He laughed. He checked her out some more, his eyes moving slow.

"Why are you looking at me like that?"

He looked so pitiful, sounded even more so. "Can I have a kiss?"

Whew. Lawd have MERCY. Danni's hormones flat out refused to cooperate with her brain. She swallowed. "Please," she replied, swallowed again. "I don't think so."

He whispered, "Why not?"

Just then she realized it, and announced, "Oh, my goodness! You're drunk."

He did this funny little snakelike side to side move with his head, and said, "So is this how it's gonna be between us from now on? No hug, at least? No nothing?"

Danni hesitated, but went ahead and gave him a hug, not because he'd asked her to, but because she wanted to, because she needed that hug, because her rebellious hormones made her do it. She had wanted to keep it brief, but he wouldn't let go. He pulled her in tighter. His breath, hot with Molson Ice, warmed her neck.

He said, "I knew you wouldn't leave me hangin'."

Then he plopped his chin on her shoulder and made a humph sound.

She told him, "You shouldn't be out here driving like this."

He gave her neck a kiss. "See how much I care? I'm out here drivin' like this for *you,* baby."

She pulled away, noticed a red tint in his eyes.

He yawned. "So," he asked, "how was work?"

Of course he thought that'd be the only place Danni would be coming from, right? "Nope," she said.

"No?" He rested back on his car, but in the very next moment he seemed uncomfortable. "What you mean, *no?*"

"Just what I said, *no.*"

"I want me another one of them hugs."

"No."

"Why not?"

"Dallas, please."

"So we just gotta stand out here? All outside like this? We can't even go up for a minute?" He looked up at her building, and then back at Danni.

"Dallas . . ."

He rolled his eyes, his eyelashes fluttering. "Yo," he said. "Maybe I am drunk."

She twirled her keys. "You think?"

He asked her, "So, who were you with tonight, Danni? What's this fool's name?"

"You don't need to know all that," she said.

"Oh, it's like that? So it is somebody else? *Sheeeiiiit*. Where he at, so I can go find his ass."

"That's the beer talking."

"I ain't drunk. Shit."

"You already said you were."

"Oh, my fault." He indulged in the humor of his own tipsiness. "That's kinda funny."

"Ha. Ha. Hee."

"Being all mean and shit. Got you a new man and shit. Yo, don't let me hold you up."

"You broke one of the rules," she notified him.

His laugh was sarcastic. "You're real funny, you know that, right? As a matter of fact, I did call first. Even called you at work today. You didn't get my messages?"

She had. Deleted 'em. Had better things to do. A cup of coffee to drink. An unimportant phone call to make. Lint balls to count. Something. Anything besides engaging her ears in words designed to alleviate his guilt-ache. He'd said *nothing* about showing up at her house, though.

"You shouldn't have come here," she told him.

"Why? Your new man might trip?"

"Maybe," she said. "But that's not the point."

"Man," he said. "You gon' tell me this fool's name or what?"

"Drive safely, Dallas, all right? Go straight home."

He stood up straight and pushed his hand out like a stop sign. "Look. I just wanted to make sure you're okay. That's it. And that's all."

"Thank you," she said. "I am."

He said, "If you want me to leave, I'm out."

She stood firm. "I already said good-bye."

He laughed in disbelief. "So leave? That's what you want me to do. Just like that?"

"Yes, I do."

"All right then," he said. He thrust his hand out for her to shake.

And she made the mistake of doing so.

And he wouldn't let go.

And she didn't try too hard to make him.

She asked him, "Are you gonna be okay to drive home?"

"This shit is all fucked up."

"I know." She tapped his arm like she would a puppy's head. "But at least you have the space you needed, right?"

"I know you don't want me to leave. Them heels would be clackin' up the damn sidewalk if you did. But it's cool. I'll holla."

• • •

"This is the best day of my life!" A woman's voice shouted, waking Danni up from her sleep the next morning. It was seven A.M. Voices, laughing and in a hurry, suddenly scurried from her clock radio at the time her alarm was always set for.

Without opening her eyes, she tried to find the snooze, but knocked a magazine onto the floor instead. Search and CoCo, the deejays who prided themselves on "paying people's bills in the A.M.," had just informed a randomly selected listener that they were going to pay off her $290 electric bill. And now, with all of the Motor City listening, the woman wanted to thank God and everyone else in the world. It was the first time in her entire life that she'd ever won anything.

Danni gave up on finding the snooze button, because that would've meant that she would have had to open her eyes, which would have meant that she would have had to wake up. And she wasn't ready to do that.

The woman was crying with joy now. "I'm diabetic, see. I needs my medicine. Last time was a mess. Went up the hill, to the post office, and was all the way back home before I knew I'd done so much as put my shoes and socks on. Thank you. So much."

She was going on and on about her diabetic stupor, and

Danni, with her eyes still tightly sealed, felt around for the cord, managed to yank before the woman did something dreadful, like break out into a song.

But still Danni didn't fall back asleep. She lay there, thinking about the day ahead of her. She needed to shower and get dressed, then cook and eat some waffles, slice a grapefruit, and have a cup of coffee, black, within forty-five minutes, had to do it in a hurry so that she would be able to slide into work, beating her coworkers in so she could work in silence for a while. She wanted to avoid as many morning greetings as she could.

Lying there comatose was not an option, no matter how tired she was. She still had to, until her adrenaline kicked in. Coffee. Real black.

The other side of the bed was empty, so she listened for a moment for the sounds of pots in the kitchen, the shower running, the television going, something. Nothing. And then she remembered that nothing was right, had been for two months, and would be indefinitely. Making love to Dallas last night had only been a dream.

She looked at her watch. Twenty minutes had passed. Her shower would have to be quick. And wait a minute, *why* had she slept in her watch?

She pulled the sheets off of herself. Danni had fallen asleep in her clothes. Her face was still sticky from tears.

She was crawling out of bed when she heard the phone ringing.

"Good morning," Ma's voice sang.

"Hey, Ma," Danni replied. "How are you?" Danni geared

herself up, prepared for the plethora of questions. *Are you coming to church on Sunday? Have you prayed yet today? Have you thanked the Lord for your blessings?*

No. No. No. No. Danni was slapping through the hangers in her closet. Nothing felt right for today. Today she needed to look vibrant, among the living. Mind over matter. She would *not* allow this breakup to break her spirit.

"Blessed." Ma didn't hesitate. "I thought about you all last night, couldn't get you off of my mind. Tried several times to call you. Couldn't sleep. Sorry to call so early."

Yeah, right. Even if she had woken Danni up, Ma would never be sorry. She was never sorry for anything.

"It's fine, Ma. I was already up."

"Shall we pray?"

Oh boy. Here we go.

"Okay," Danni sighed.

"Sure?"

"Positive."

"You don't sound like it."

"Well, I am."

"Well, praise be." Ma took a long breath and was quiet for a few deliberate moments. "Father God we come to you . . ."

Careful not to make a sound as she did, Danni gathered a fluffy fresh towel and her kiwi-cucumber shower gel, and placed them on the bathroom sink. Not that she didn't believe in prayer, not that she wasn't listening, but this had been a constant all her life.

When Danni was sixteen years old, she and Kizzy had spent all week at Northland Mall trying to find the perfect green pumps to go with Danni's homecoming dress, a pair that the small amount of money the two of them had saved could pay for. And when the huge day arrived and Danni was getting ready, there Ma stood in the doorway, looking somber and concerned. Danni kept plucking the curlers out of her hair regardless.

"You know," Ma had said. "With having to buy your school supplies last month—"

"It's okay, Ma," Danni had smiled. "Me and Kiz used our babysitting money. Mrs. Frank gave me a little extra last week."

Ma raised her chin and squinted her eyes. "Oh?"

"Just," Danni clarified, "ten dollars extra, Ma. It wasn't much."

"I see. Well, don't waste it. You'll need lunch money next week."

"I know, Ma," Danni replied.

No have fun tonight. No let me get a picture of you before you go. No who are you even going with. None of that. Oh, but a prayer. Right then, right there. *Father God we thank you for the roof over our heads, for the air we breathe, for the ground that we walk upon* . . . Danni was thankful, of course she was. Ma *had* given her a home, but just for once, just one time, could she not be reminded of how *thankful* she was supposed to be? Couldn't she just pretend that she was entitled to belong for once?

That was back in the day when Ma ran a small Bible study

group out of her basement. Please. Now she had a seven-hundred-member congregation in Ypsilanti.

Danni eased her candy-apple red pantsuit from a hanger as she listened to Ma ask God to build a fortress of protection around her. She eventually concluded with, "All praises, all praises. Amen."

"Amen," Danni said. "Thank you."

Then Ma asked Danni about work.

"Can't complain." Danni dared not. Ma knew N'Drea, had gotten Danni that gig at ReveNations. "Big opening reception tonight."

"Well, praise be," Ma said. "Well, just so you know, Shirley Caesar is going to be in Cleveland the last weekend of next month. We're taking the van and driving over."

Ever since she'd finished that free Internet class at the library, Ma had constantly been finding things, had even started building a Web site for her progressive spiritual group—Ladies of Praise.

Their current ministry was reaching out to abusive men, combing the shelters asking battered women how to contact their spouses or boyfriends so they could go out to pray with the men. It was unnerving at first, to know that she and her group of spiritualist friends were out there knocking on random doors, asking violent men if they could pray with them. But most of their visits had been met with peace. That a soft or kind word could turn away wrath was their motto, and apparently it worked most of the time.

"Sounds nice. I'll get back to you on that," Danni replied.

"Let me know."

Danni cradled the phone as she ironed her pants. "Where is everyone? The house is so quiet."

"Still asleep. School's out, you know."

"How's DeMarco?"

"Oh, that child. Summer school."

"He flunked something?"

"Algebra. Counselor said he's gotta pass it to graduate next year. No room in his schedule in the fall."

"Really?"

"I don't know what we're gonna do with him."

Danni scrunched up her eyebrows. "What do you mean?"

"Gotta tell him two hundred times every morning to wake up. He don't wanna go . . . How's my girl?"

"Kizzy's fine."

"Tell her I've been praying for her, prayin' that one glorious Sunday morning I'll look up, and there she'll be, comin' up the aisle. Praise His name. God's gonna do it."

"She'll come eventually, I'm sure," Danni said.

"You, too. Haven't seen you sitting out there in a couple of months now. Next month is our women's week."

Danni looked at her watch. "Oh?"

"You sound distracted."

"I'm sorry Ma. I'm running late for work."

"Well, don't let me hold you."

Danni said, "I love you, Ma."

"Love *you*."

Danni threw the cordless on the bed, and went into the kitchen.

Instinctively, she had an image of Dallas sitting at the kitchen counter in his robe, watching the morning news and sipping a glass of juice. He'd look up, see her. "Dream about me?" he used to say.

As a matter of fact, she had.

She thought of how she used to brush her hand along his forearm, the tattoo of a black panther, right before she would lean in for a morning kiss.

But then she took that imaginary paintbrush, broke it in half, and tossed the pieces over her shoulder.

No way, no how was she gonna stay in this funk.

By the time Danni filled a thermos with orange juice and tossed a raisin bagel into a baggie, she was feeling so optimistic that she was humming out loud. She searched all over for her keys, which took an additional ten minutes, and then she remembered how she had hurled them across the room when she'd come in last night. She found them on the floor in her bedroom.

Just like that randomly selected listener, Danni had decided that today was going to feel like the best day of her life. Not because of what someone did for her, rather because of what she was going to do for herself.

She would make tonight's reception unbelievable. She would work hard preparing until noon, and then would have a precelebration by treating herself to lunch at a five-star restaurant. Maybe she'd even ask Garvey to join her. Or maybe she'd go alone. Maybe she'd wait and do it tomorrow, after the fact. She'd drive down to Toledo, treat herself to that sensational restaurant downtown, called Diva.

She would dine with the power to her cell phone turned off, *without* a newspaper or anything else to read. She'd ask for the dinner menu when she got to the restaurant, eat whatever she wanted, even the bread and butter that she usually passed on. She would smile back at neighboring tables, nosy folks that were looking over at her every few minutes to see if anyone had joined her yet. Maybe she'd get *real* bold and would even ask the hostess to remove the other chair. She would dine alone, and be comfortable, proud even. She would allow herself to be intrigued, in awe of her own thoughts.

She grabbed her purse off the coffee table, and just as she did, she saw the sea of stones. Untouched since Saturday morning. They'd be there later, she reminded herself, if she wanted to try again. Right now she needed to get to work, the big reception tonight.

Danni had locked her door and was all the way down the hallway before she realized that she'd left that bagel right there on the kitchen counter.

"Oh well," she said out loud as she waited for the elevator.

"*Buenos días,*" Bumpy said when Danni joined her on the elevator.

Danni smiled. "Oh, good morning."

Bumpy wiped the sweat off of her face, from underneath her eyeglasses. "Such a beautiful smile you have."

"Nothing's gonna steal my joy, Bumpy. I won't let it."

Bumpy sighed. "I could use your energy. It gets so lonely, you see, without *mi amor*."

This reminded Danni. "That song you play all the time, Bumpy, what is it?"

"Oh." Bumpy knew exactly which song Danni was referring to, and pulled her fist to her chest, her insides swelling with joy. "'Vida Es un Carnaval.' It was our song. He and I. It still is."

"I figured it must be special. I hear it so much."

"You like? I could burn it for you."

Danni nodded graciously. Really she'd just wanted to know the story behind the song. She didn't know Spanish very well. "Oh, but then you'd have to translate it for me," she said.

Bumpy looked thrilled. "Oh, that'd be okay. But, really, it's all the same. Feelings, even if you don't speak the language. Life is a carnival, no?"

Danni smiled. Indeed it was.

• • •

She was driving in a zone, possessed by a trance of memories and wondering, weaving her car up I-75. She eased up on the gas pedal and sighed, so glad that she had come to her senses before some lights and a siren came chasing. The last thing she needed was another speeding ticket, for her insurance man to leave yet another one of his friendly messages about—"unfortunately and with regret"—needing to raise her damn premium.

She looked up. Her exit was right there. She had to cross two lanes of morning traffic in two seconds. She held her breath and tried to remember Ma's old saying, something about God looking out for fools and babies.

By the time Danni pulled up at the gallery, her mask was in place and she felt emotionally ready to pretend again. She saw Garvey's bicycle, already chained to the pole, but she didn't see N'Drea's Cadillac. That was unusual.

Danni walked into the gallery and her eyes had to adjust to the abrupt brightness. She was not suffocated by the lingering trail of N'Drea's perfume as she usually was. Strange. Danni *and* Garvey had beat N'Drea in that morning? The day of the VIP reception? Even stranger.

"What are you doing, trying to catch a worm?" Garvey stood in the doorway of Danni's office. "Miss Early Bird."

Danni looked up from her computer keys, where she had only just begun pecking one hesitant word at a time. Maybe she should've been honest yesterday with N'Drea, told her that she needed help with the speech.

She took the pencil out of her mouth, frowned at all of the teeth marks, and told him, "Yeah, I had to come in early today."

"I see," he said. "Me too. Had to print out a paper for class."

"Have a seat."

He sat down in front of her. "I don't know. I feel a little strange, don't you? You, me, and the intern beat N'Drea into work today. Something's up." He waited a moment. "Her office was dark, so it's not like she came and ran back out or something."

"That is weird. But maybe she's just running late. Hey, did you pick up the *Press?*"

"Uh," he stroked his goatee. "I take it you haven't."

"What's wrong?"

"Well."

"*What* happened?"

"Nothing in the events calendar for this weekend."

"*No?*" Danni cringed. "Are you serious?"

"Very."

"Well, what happened?"

He shrugged. "I don't know."

Danni shook her head. "I know the media advisory went out. I followed up weeks ago."

"I remember."

"That's weird," Danni said. "The events blurb always runs the day of the private opening."

"I know. N'Drea's gonna scream. I'm sorry."

"Not your fault, Garvey," Danni said. "I'm sure it won't be that big of a deal. The ads start on Thursday. At least *that* will run in time for the weekend."

"Let me get this straight. We almost had a major misprint. *And that's okay?*" He laughed. "I'm stayin' away from the water up in here."

"Well, it's not *okay* per se." Danni shrugged. "But it's not that big of a deal. Right?"

He frowned up like there was a bad smell lurking. "Let's hope. I dunno."

"Garvey, stop it."

Danni's phone buzzed.

"Good morning Ms. Blair," the intern piped in. "Mr. Lay-lock. Line three."

Like Danni really had time or patience for *him* right now. She quickly replied back, "Voice mail please? Thanks."

Garvey sat up. "Still dissin' the man you swore you were gonna marry someday. I think maybe I might need to take you on over to the emergency room. Have 'em run a CAT scan, or *somethin'*."

"Oh, please."

"How long has it been since you started putting your dozens-of-lilies-a-week-sending prince through to your voice mail?"

"Doesn't matter."

"Still not trying to go back to paradise, huh?"

"I took a one-way flight *out* of paradise. Okay? Remember?"

"Still no second thoughts?"

"But then there's always a third." She showed him how pearly her whites were.

"Well, all right . . ."

Just that quick, the intern chimed in again. "Ms. Blair?"

"Yes?"

"Another call. A Miss Kizzy Murphy."

Danni hummed a laugh, shook her head. "I'll pick up."

"Line two," the intern informed her.

"Kizzy," Danni said into the phone, swiveled around to study the suede wallpaper while she talked. "Nicole's been popping out babies every year. I think you should accept that Eddie Murphy's marriage probably is going to last."

"I know." Kizzy giggled. "But, girl, I just got finished with a *Boomerang* and *Raw* marathon last night. Remember Jesse Jackson's tried-and-true slogan? Well, hope is still alive."

Danni leaned back her chair, and whirled back around to face Garvey. "Do you mind?" Then she said to Kizzy, "So, what's up?"

"Got some scoop," Kizzy told her. "Want it?"

"Scoop it like ice cream," Danni replied. "What's up?"

"About Dallas."

"Aw, Kiz. Is this really necessary?"

"I just thought you should know, that's all."

"Well, hurry up. We have that reception tonight. Things are hectic."

"I figured something was up. You didn't call me back last night. Have you heard from him?"

"Who?"

"Laylock."

"Oh." Danni toyed with the phone cord. "Not really, why?"

"She's one of the team doctors."

"She *who?*"

"Some Bonjour bitch."

"Excuse me?"

"I guess she speaks French."

"And we're discussing a bilingual woman because . . . ?"

"I guess she and Dallas are dating. At least that's what I hear, girl."

Danni sat still and focused on the window. "A doctor?"

"Yes. And that ain't all."

Danni could hear water splashing. More than likely Kizzy was probably in a bubble bath, relaxing with her morning glass of juice.

Kizzy took a breath. "You want it straight or coated?"

He was going to marry her. Danni sat up straight and prepared for the jolt. "Give it to me raw. The whole 411."

Kizzy spoke in a dispatcher's tone. "Biracial. Half sista, half milk. Went to some fancy bullshit college in France. I guess that's why she's bilingual. Anyhow, originally from South Africa. Five nine and bangin'. Drives a Benz. No kids. Travels with the team occasionally."

"Bullshit."

"Yup."

"Travels with the team?"

"That's what I hear, girl."

Danni took a deep breath. "I must be a closet masochist or something. Why'd I even let you tell me this? Damn."

"Yeah, I know," Kizzy said. "So forget everything I said the other day. Maybe it is good that you're *not* sweatin' his ass."

"See."

"*And* there's a maraschino for the top."

"What?"

"Sure?"

"Wound is opened now, pour on the salt."

"She and Mr. Laylock were spotted over at Fishbones last night, doin' the red beans and rice thang."

"Last night?"

"Last night."

"Just the two of them?"

"I guess. Why?"

"Well, supposedly a bunch of folks were out for Rock's birthday—one of their trainers."

"Oh."

"So maybe this woman just happened to be there."

"Right, right . . . *maybe*."

"Who'd you find all this out from?"

"Mike Lothery. The catch is, I've gotta have lunch with him. I know his ass is gonna pick some spot where everybody's gonna see us too."

Mike Lothery was a sports journalist, had been trying to interview Kizzy on a personal level for years. And for years, Kizzy had been using him for press access to events that he was too busy to attend. He drove a Chevrolet Malibu. Kizzy dated absolutely nothing below a Lincoln, and even *that* was pushing it.

Danni sighed. "Poor Mike."

"Yeah, well, don't sweat the international bitch, all right? Be breezy."

"Always. Gotta be."

"I already know she ain't no cuter than you," Kizzy added. "I don't give a damn *who* they say she looks like. And she ain't no smarter, I don't care what expensive-ass university she went off to. She could be a damn scientist."

Danni knew that Kizzy was just trying to spare her feelings. No way would Kizzy have ever said anything different. The woman might have even looked like a supermodel, like Naomi, or Tyra, or even Shawni Baldwin, and Kizzy would've still assured Danni that she had no reason to feel threatened.

"Please," Danni said. "Hey. Nobody determines my happiness, but me."

"I know that's right, girl."

"There was a time in my life when I didn't know him, you know. I was okay then, and I'll be fine now."

"Right, right . . ."

"All I've gotta do is stay focused on other things."

"I know that's right."

"I've gotta keep on keepin' on."

"Keep on, keep on, girl."

Danni swiveled her chair back around, and rolled her eyes when she saw Garvey still lingering in the hallway, reading the same notices on the bulletin board that he'd been reading for weeks. Danni told Kizzy she had to go, that she'd call her later, and when she hung up she saw the red light blinking.

Dallas took a very long breath. "It's me," his voice on the message said. "Hit me up. I was trippin' last night. One too many, know what I'm sayin'. I still wanna take you to lunch, a'ight? We do need to talk."

She pressed seven. Message deleted.

And then she buzzed the intern.

"Yes, Miss Blair?"

"Uh, in a little bit, would you mind putting in a lunch order for me? My usual Chinese? I'll be dining in for lunch again, thanks."

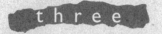

three

12:01 a.m.

Danni really just wanted to get this shit over with. That evening, the air in the gallery felt dense, stagnant like a forgotten attic. And to make things even more unpleasant, the chair she was sitting on was rickety. Like the room full of people sitting in front of her, she felt jaded by the unpleasant wait.

She kept tugging at her bun, keeping an incessant eye on the door. Any second now Roman Bilal had better slither his ungrateful ass through that door.

At last he granted the room the honor of his presence, strolled in looking like some neo—soul musician with a hangover. The expression on his face said that he didn't give a damn if he was twenty minutes late. Looked like an angry Lenny Kravitz.

Great. Another pompous jerk deemed artistic prodigy.

He looked young enough to be a graduate student. Who did he think he was? It wasn't until he stood in front of her and finally whispered, "I apologize for the delay," that Danni didn't feel the need to roll her eyes at him. At least he'd apologized.

From the back of the room, N'Drea gave Danni the okay, and Danni cleared her throat and approached the podium beside the easel, now draped in black, withholding the piece.

Danni had long since decided to speak the language of their guests, to do just what N'Drea would've done. She rattled off his credentials, asked for their warm welcome via applause, and gave him the floor.

His fingers combed their way through his untamed hair, and he rubbed his hands along his sideburns, stopped mid-cheek, and sighed. After an irritated glance, he disregarded the podium, stepped away from the microphone

Sitting right up front was N'Drea, surrounded by a group of uppity yuppies, the women with their hair in either some gorgeous dreadlocks or a chic natural, and it was pretty much the same for the fellas, with the exception of one who appeared to be conservative.

The room had been engaged in a buzz characteristic of a first day of class, nervous small talk spiked with artificial laughter. Most of the patrons seemed to be familiar with one another. Danni had seen the president of the Urban League come in, gave some dap to Mayor Kilpatrick, and waved at a few of N'Drea's networking partners who were scattered throughout the room. It was a nice crowd.

Now they were close-lipped and still.

He folded his arms across his chest, tucked his hands under his pits, and his voice was calm.

"If you came out tonight because you wanted to learn, welcome." He went to the back of the room and flipped the lights off, and then there was the clamorous click of a slide projector. Its light hungrily illuminated the room, its focus became the black cloth, and, on cue, Danni removed it. The canvas was stark white, untouched, and waiting.

After her eyes adjusted, Danni saw the first clip, a close-up image of a younger, less stressed Roman Bilal wearing a green Kangol, a silly smirk on his face.

"This was a long time ago," he said. "It was the night of the Def Jam concert. Run DMC, Whodini, LL Cool J, Doug E. Fresh. But for a militant, righteous cat like myself, all that mattered was Public Enemy. Others were holdin' their laceless shell toes in the air. I was pumping my fist. 911 was a joke to me too, know what I'm sayin'?"

That picture spoke to Danni like a postcard from the eighties, an era when things were so much more fun. Even for her.

He corrected Danni's thoughts. "For me, those were trying times. A father who used to roll with Geronimo Pratt, doing time for his convictions, cared less about his seed. My mother couldn't handle it, got some help from the pipe."

The slide changed, and the picture seemed to have bled. It

was him, same pose, same silly grin, but it wasn't film anymore. Now it was a watercolor self-portrait, more amplified, more definite colors. And he looked angrier.

"When I was coming up," he reported, "fun was for punks. I had to have a mission, every day a goal. Didn't help that I had a no-shit-taking grandfather who was too sharp for his own wit. Times had changed too much, and there wasn't no way in the world that he was accepting that.

"A man's integrity, not the gold rope chains around his neck, should be his honor. Bebop and jazz, now that was music. Rap wasn't nothing but shit-talking to a studio beat.

"Streets was raising my cats. Only place my grandfather let me go was one block over, the Sammy Davis Jr. Community Center.

"At first I hated it, wanted to just play Calico in a basement like the rest of my cats. Then I met this older cat, Shahir, listened to Chuck D., and I latched on. Bebop might as well have been Swahili to me. Fight the power, know what I'm sayin'?

"Shock, uh, the name we gave him, was organizing vigils, rallies, leading hunger strikes, stuff my father used to write to me about doing in his heyday. Shock was my Malcolm X, my Huey Newton.

"He never made me go outside, go play kickball, he just would give me a stack of leaflets, tell me to fold, make the creases tight, sayin' that appearance is everything. I kept wishing my pops could see.

"Shock gave me my first brushes. Told me to make the canvas show the world what I felt.

"Folks all around me was gettin' blowed. Dabbling, watching the colors blend, swirl together made me feel what they bragged about, that head-nodding oblivion my cats swore felt better than pussy."

He came back to the front of the room and retrieved a green apple from his brown leather attaché. The light from the projector allowed the audience, sitting erect like a private-school class, to watch as he pulled a tiny red knife from the bag as well, as he began to peel. He ate it, one crunch at a time, and talked as he did.

"I wanna know why you're here. Forget raising your hand if you got something to say, let it flow."

The conservative one, with his elbow resting on the arm of his chair, pointed his finger to the sky. "Well, I for one couldn't resist the blurb in *The South End*. I'm actually premed, but I do have a deep appreciation. This is great stuff, man. All respect."

"Hold on, my brotha, hold on." Roman shook his head. "We are all my artists, all God's children. Thugs, nerds, pastors, and hoes. *We're all* storytellers. Everyone. Writers use words. Your average cat, like my grandfather, uses oral tradition. Go right on over there to General Motors, a Ford plant, listen to the pulse. The history. Stories, laughin', jokin', and jivin'. The characters you see. All God's children, tellin' stories, tellin' tales. Passin' it on. Art.

"M'man Kirk Whalum with his horn. Jordan on the court, an epic that nobody wanted to end. Poetry in the air.

"So don't doubt your story. You owe it to God to find your vessel for telling it, your medium.

"Mind you," he said, "this is not to be confused with theme. Theme is the bottom line, the snapshot. Story is much more. It's the movement before the picture was snapped, the morning after the first time you got some, not just the sex. Story is the experience."

Danni had stopped twitching, her chair was quiet now.

Roman returned to the back of the room and swapped the slide.

Magnified now on the wall in front of them was another picture, another watercolor portrait. It was a little boy, around seven or eight years old, with ashy brown skin, wearing a white T-shirt and a pair of untied and dirty tennis shoes. Huge buildings towered around him, but he was captivated by something inside his hand, by its shining brilliance.

His nose was running, he had a scar on his left knee, but the viewer couldn't see what was in his hand. Danni knew that had been the artist's intent.

While they gazed at the painting, Roman's voice strolled through the story. At first he spoke so low that Danni had to strain to hear.

"My grandfather thought he knew about money, kept feedin' me this lesson about coins and paper bills, how they really represent gold; said that we exchange coins and bills for goods, that paper and the coins wasn't worth shit. It's what they represent that's the true master of the economy, the damn czar of every country. Said that people somehow forgot over the years that paper and coins aren't nothing, just some damn mobilized symbols for what still holds the ultimate value. *Gold.*"

All that could be heard was an occasional sound of him chewing that fresh apple.

When he decided that he damn well felt like it, he started talking again.

"So, being the Michael-Evans-on-*Good-Times* type of cat that I was," he said, "the next day, my chest all puffed out, I marched myself down to the bank with four quarters, waited in line, and smacked 'em on the damn counter. Said, I don't want these here coins. I'd like to have my gold, please.

"You'd have thought somebody was back there tickling that sista's feet, the way she hollered, kicking her leg, laughing and carrying on. 'Ain't that cute,' she said. Then she goes and calls her little coworker over.

"And they wouldn't shut up, all that laughing. One of 'em gave me a Dum-Dum and a stack of money holders. Told me I'd have to save a lot more money for even a slither. Pissed me off. On top of that, it was lemon. *Watermelon* was my thing.

"I had just been loving this idea. I would actually be able to go to Toys 'R' Us, buy a race car or something, with a real live hunk of gold.

"And all I got to leave with were those quarters? Man, it was like the day I found out that there really wasn't no street named Sesame where I could get on my bike, ride and find Big Bird."

Danni wanted to laugh, but didn't want to miss hearing a word if she did, so she held it in.

He continued, "On my way home I got in on a pickup game of baseball, played second base, enough to make me forget. I was a kid. Eight, I think.

"Years later, I started to wonder, wanted to ask somebody who in the hell had been given the power to say that even gold was worth shit."

The room erupted with approval and laughter, claps and cheers from even the dignitaries, even N'Drea.

He continued, "So I unveiled this painting a few years ago at the Art Tatum community center where I grew up. A lot has changed since Shock and his crew faded away. Only four people came out.

"There was this woman up front, said she thought that the meaning was hope. Hope. One word. She pointed out his dirty clothes, said that there was still so much within his reach regardless of being broke, so much *hope* she said.

"Was she correct? I think maybe, as far as theme. Is it the story? No. I just told you the story."

And then he made his way back up to the front of the room, back into the light, and asked, "Anyone else? I'd like to hear from others. What brought you here tonight?"

There was so much energy prickling throughout her, and Danni thought that that feeling was so much better than anything she'd ever felt. She was affected, immobilized, in such a fresh way. It felt surreal.

She tried to look away. Couldn't. Was in a trance. She was floating, flying while sitting right there in her chair. An old friend was calling, whispering her name. She felt connected to something, wasn't sure what, but she leaned forward and wanted to concentrate. The room was pretty quiet, but the occasional rustling of the programs, a quiet cough, or even a sniff, was too loud for Danni right now.

Roman Bilal's expression was patient now, some of the intensity had drained from his face. He looked more relaxed.

"You in the back," he said. "You wanna speak?"

"Why am I here," the woman began. "My job."

A few people chuckled and voiced their agreements.

The woman continued, "But I used to be creative, one of those people who was just *on, all* of the time. I was involved, inquisitive about the world, so hungry. Life said 'on your mark, get set,' and then I started shutting down."

Roman wanted to make good and sure that she was finished, so he waited. She was.

So then, with a nod, he communicated that he understood. "My beautiful sista, that's all right," he said.

It was like a voice from the heavens had told her what she really, even desperately, needed to hear. She closed her eyes, nodded, and whispered a thank-you.

He nodded at Danni.

She tried to remember the real reason she was sitting up there, what her next cue was, but couldn't.

Roman Bilal tried to play it off with a closed-teeth smile. He looked around the room again. "Anyone else . . . ? Anyone," he said.

Comments poured throughout the room for a long while, and then he took the initiative himself and announced to them that they could feel free to enjoy the refreshments, to please take the opportunity to get to know someone else on a more personal level, to share more stories, that he'd hang out for a while.

"Yes." Danni snapped to and stood up. "Please do. There's plenty of wine, cheese . . ."

While a lot of people headed outside for fresh air or to puff on a cigarette, Danni made her way back to him. The closer she got, the more embarrassed she felt.

Standing close to him now, she realized that his face was more flawed than had appeared from the back, a couple of aged acne marks on his nut-brown leather-looking skin, a few dark freckles sprinkled across his nose.

"I'm sorry," she said. "I was so invested in what you were saying. *Very* interesting."

"I'm glad you were blessed," he replied.

"I was." Danni eased herself onto the edge of the stage. "So are you a full-time artist?"

"Not even close," he said. "Ever heard of The Office?"

The only place Danni knew of called The Office was a trendy new lounge, a couple of blocks over. "You're not talking about that new bar?"

He corrected her, was apparently mocking someone when he said, "Actually, it's an *evening cocktail lounge*. But, yeah."

She laughed. "I've heard of it."

"Nothing but the same old shit with nicer tables and better lighting, if you ask me." He danced his fingers along an imaginary row of something, and Danni watched, admiring his braided leather bracelet, intrigued by the visible strength in his hands. All his jewelry, even the ring on his thumb, appeared handcrafted.

He asked her, "What do you drink?"

Danni gave him a questionable look. "Don't even tell me you're a bartender?"

"I could say that, but I'd be lying." He ran his fingers along again. "I can mix it up, whatever you'd like."

Danni giggled, played along. "Okay then, Mr. Bartender Man, how about a Pepsi?"

He thought for a moment. "How about a Coca-Cola?"

"Ginger ale?"

"With rum?"

"No, thanks. Straight, no ice."

He stood there, waiting for the punch line. "Just a soda?"

She nodded. "I try not to drink. I like to experience things fully, as few influences as possible."

He thought about that. He pretended to grab a glass, filled it with ice. Then he remembered her request, and pretended to pour it back out. "Spoken like a true artist," he said.

"Thanks," she told him after he slid her the imagined glass. "I've never been there though, The Office."

"Nothing but a bunch of key-chain flashers."

Danni had no clue what he meant, and he could tell.

He changed his voice to a more nasal tone. "Hi, I'm Sam." He dangled his fingers, his nails clean and freshly filed, in front of her face. "Watch closely. Be hypnotized by my BMW or Ferrari key chain."

She realized what he was getting at, and found that amusing. "Funny," she said.

"That's what I say. That's live, that you don't drink."

"Well, thank you."

"Cats constantly trying to outdo each other, gettin' worse with every shot of Hen. It's wild. But I enjoy what I do, listening, hearing what folks have to say."

"Oh."

"Why the raised eyebrows?"

"I just thought, you know . . . With your bio, your education . . ."

"All my money from my art goes to the center. All my education goes to my people. I bartend to eat."

"That's so impressive."

"I teach workshops for free."

"Are you serious?"

"Only ninety-nine percent of the time. Right now, yes."

"And the pieces you sell?"

"I make checks out to the Sammy Davis Jr. Community Center of Detroit. Gotta give life back."

"I bet they appreciate that. I'm sure they need it."

"Put it like this, a concert over at the Joe Louis can sell out as long as they're cussing, talking about money, cars, and bitches. I brought some cats in from Hampton and Harvard to talk about applying to college, some engineering scholarships . . ."

"Don't tell me . . ."

"Nuff said."

"No kids?"

"Oh, we drew a few," he said. "But just the choir, sayin' amen to the preacher."

Danni had insisted to the cosmos for years that if she could sell one piece of work, get some whisper of assurance that her sketches mattered, could get a big fat lump sum of money, she'd freeze-frame her dimples, blow ReveNations a farewell kiss, travel the world, dancing in the streets with no music playing, constantly creating.

And he was working at a bar despite all of that?

She told him, "I just always thought that once you start selling your work, that if you're gonna be an artist, you could, or rather should just focus on the art, on creating. Totally. Completely."

"You say that like, if you want to fly to the moon, you should just start flappin' your arms. Not that easy. Damn for sure isn't that financially consistent. What, forty, fifty thousand dollars here and there is gonna move me on up like the Jeffersons? Gonna make everything be all right? For the rest of my life? For all my people?"

He shook his head. "I can go around, talk some art into all these yuppies, but meanwhile we've got thousands of kids all across, the kids that won't ever know about Jean-Michel Basquiat, Elizabeth Catlett, Robert Colescott. I'd rather put that money where it can fester, feed the mind of a future Jacob Lawrence or the next Romare Bearden. I'm hungry for that."

He caught a glimpse of the look on her face. "I'm not one of those cats, just as long as I've got a damn brush in my hand, I'll eat boiled water for soup."

She blushed a smile, extended her hand. "It is *such* a pleasure to meet you."

He gasped, shook her hand, cupped it, and let out a laugh. "You say that like I'm the president."

"No," she said. "Your vibe is just so refreshing."

He asked, "So what's yours?"

Danni had to think for a moment, now that the focus was on her. "Okay, well, my vibe is pretty simple. I have an associate's in art, which basically, you know, all that means is that I didn't have some job in corporate America lined up for me after graduation. You know how it goes, no ads in the paper that read 'talented artist wanted. Start immediately. Competitive pay. Great benefits.'" She giggled. He didn't even smile.

"Yeah," he said. "So what else?"

"So." She decided to continue despite what appeared to be his sudden visible disinterest, like he was thinking about something else while she talked. "After I finished college I had to subject myself to working at a home improvement store for a while to save up some cash to move."

He nodded. "Oh."

"And then, just like the three thousand other artists who were sharing my same vision and making that same trek about every single day of the year, I moved to the Big Apple, all of us loaded with a lethal amount of hope, armed with nothing but a bunch of artistic dreams."

"No kidding? You lived in the good old Mecca for artists?"

"Queens. Astoria."

"Did Brooklyn for a while myself."

"I read that in your bio."

Sometimes it was refreshing to remind her own self of how far she'd advanced since those days, so Danni sighed at the memories, and continued, "Not even a fast-food joint would give me a job. So when my savings ran out I had to cut short my fancy stint as a big-city artist. Left while I could still afford a one-way flight. Came back here, Ma found me this gig. And here I am."

"How 'bout that?"

"That's right."

And Danni wondered if some aspect of her rambling had intrigued him, or if he was just lost in his own thoughts.

Then he asked, "So what'd you do, just spin the globe and pick Detroit?"

"I'm from here. Plus, it's okay. Enough culture to keep me content. But I always thought eventually I'd move again, get back out there after I saved up some money."

"What happened?"

"Fell in love."

"Ah," he said. "Money and love. The world would be still without those two."

"Isn't that the truth," she agreed. "But I'm sure I'll move again someday, when the money is right. Why'd you leave New York?"

"My roots called me back. I wanted to water the grounds I grew up on."

"Oh."

"And," he admitted, "love."

"Uh-huh."

"So how long have you been with the gallery?"

"Three years." She glanced around, noticed the people lingering, waiting to speak with him. She whispered, "It's like being a chef and working for one of the finest restaurants imaginable, but all you get to do is put other chefs' food on a plate and serve it. The caviar starts to just be raw fish, the crème brûlée just looks like crusted pudding. It's work every day, trying not to abandon your own soul."

He rubbed his hand along his sideburns. "That's deep." His eyes gave a quick study to her pearl studs, her red silk blouse, designer slacks, her red strappy sandals.

She smiled. "Don't look like the artistic type, I know."

He looked amused. "Well, that too."

"Too?"

She waited.

He said, "You're elegant. I dig that."

Danni didn't say a word, just made a *hmm* sound.

Their conversation had begun to feel like a good first date where neither one of them wanted to fake a stomachache to get out of coffee afterward. But she had to remind herself where she was, what she was doing there, who he was, and that there were people waiting. And he appeared, Danni noticed, to be doing the same.

Danni looked around the room. "People are waiting to meet you."

He looked her in the eyes.

"Those slides," Danni added real quick and was able to, in

one blink, still picture that little boy squinting, that green Kangol, that silly grin. She exhaled her amazement. "You're awesome, Roman. Potential to be huge. Serious skills."

He twisted his lips, gave her a come-on-now look, and said, "Like I said, it's not about the money. I'm here to give.

"Plus," he added, "skills are everyday. Any man with too much time on his hands can work hard and hone some skills. I got *gifts*. I'm already hip that the world doesn't always know what to do with gifts. Look at all the true warriors. Nobody gave a damn until they had died, most of 'em broke. Fuck fame."

She playfully looked him up and down. "Scared of you."

He was amused by her humor, and her chosen response seemed to relax him again.

He told her, "But I do appreciate your homage to the slides. That's respect."

"Right, well, let me go . . ."

"So you create." He stopped her.

"I do. I'm a painter."

"Skills? Or gifts?"

Danni looked over, caught a glare from N'Drea, her cropped natural gelled back sleek tonight, and she was dressed in all silver. She approached Danni and Roman Bilal with her nose so far in the air you could measure the length of her neck.

"So sorry to interrupt." N'Drea linked her arm in and whispered to Roman, as if Danni wasn't even standing there. Then she gave Danni a wide-eyed phony-ass grin. "Garvey's looking for you. Something about the wine."

"I was just getting ready to go check on everything," Danni replied.

N'Drea nudged Roman. "Powerful presentation."

"Thank you, my sista," he replied.

"And you know," N'Drea said, "I'm quite familiar with that community center myself. I had an uncle who was a Panther too, probably knew your dad. And I've heard of Shahir, he used to be *really* involved in the community, if I'm not mistaken?"

"Rest his soul, sho nuff."

N'Drea shook her head. "And I considered Howard, but I chose Spelman."

He grinned. "Good school."

N'Drea noticed Danni still standing there, watching. "Did Danni tell you who her boyfriend was?"

He looked at Danni, shook his head, no smile. "We didn't discuss that, no."

Danni didn't answer, couldn't believe N'Drea. As usual, always trying to remind Danni that a mainstream-looking square would always have a hard time fitting in with ethnic-looking holes.

"The Piston. Uh, what's his name? Detroit, uh, *Dallas* Laylock that is," N'Drea said. "You know, the basketball star."

He got his eye at Danni, visible surprise on his face. "Sho nuff?"

"Right," Danni could fake a smile, too, and did. "I really need to go find Garvey."

Danni started walking away, but waved back. "Nice meeting you, Roman." She upheld her smile.

To answer his question though, Danni had gifts.

. . .

Someone asked Danni once why she was an artist. Not because it's cool, not because she aspired to be some chic, bohemian sophisticate who was in tune with herself. It's just that sometimes, every once in a while, when she allowed herself to remember, the memories were too much, the canvas her only release. All her life, since the first time she held a paintbrush in the second grade, Danni created because she had to. At first it was paintings of various things she saw: a pretty flower or a cute dog. But the older she got, the more she understood that colors create mood, that the magic of creating was painting not necessarily what was there but what you actually saw.

Danni had thrown a T-shirt over her clothes, was standing in her living room, the room lit by the late-evening moon. Sade's voice was pouring a rhythmic narcotic out from her stereo's speakers, and a cup of steaming hazelnut decaf was within Danni's reach. Danni's mind had been consumed by blending images, unclear memories, and ideas—one in particular was quite stimulating.

She poured two tones of paint onto her palette. Black, because it was unmistakable, and white, because any dilution would be obvious. Either people love you, or they don't. Either they stay, or they leave. No more shades of gray. In fact—she reached for a yellow stone, now good and dry—perhaps she should start again, paint over a few.

Pzzzz. Pzzzz. She could hear the vibration coming from her purse, from her cell phone, and she thought about not answering. She didn't even need to, she already knew. Kizzy. She reached over on the mantel, slipped her hand in her purse, and flipped open the phone.

"Hey," she answered.

"Danni, it's me," Kizzy said. "Buzz me up."

Danni looked down at her paintbrush and sighed. She snatched the remote. Channel 105. And there was Kiz.

"Come on, girl." Kizzy smiled into the camera.

Great. Danni dropped her brush into the mayonnaise jar, went over to the door, and pushed down on the white button by the door before she cracked it open. She went to the freezer, pulled out an ice tray, grabbed two glasses, and pulled two cans of Diet Vernor's out from the pantry.

Danni pushed away her stack of magazines on the dining-room table, *Vanity Fair, Cosmo,* and *Vibe,* and put down the glasses. By the time Kizzy came in, Danni had filled both of the glasses, had copped a squat, and was waiting.

"What's up, girl?" Kizzy's flip-flops flipped and flopped as she made her way over to the table and hung her trendy hobo bag on the back of the chair.

"Hey," Danni replied.

"Just came back from over at MGM. You know, figured since I was just around the corner I'd check on you, girl."

"I'm cool. Who'd you go with?"

"Your hair looks cute. I like the bun. Classic. This Wall Street brotha I met at the mall. In town for the week. Talkin' about he wanted me to be his good-luck charm by the craps table. If his ass would've hit big, oh I'd have been some good luck all right. So, what's up?"

Danni eyed the damp paint stains on her thumb. "Nothing. Not much."

"I didn't know if you were tripping over the bonjour bitch or not, so I said, let me go on over here and check on my sister girl."

Danni leaned back and slouched in her chair. "I'm cool. It'd be nice to get away though. Someplace quiet. Indiana or something—"

"Indi-*who*. Girl, for what?"

Danni let out a very long breath. "I was vibin' with this guy, our artist, a real deep brotha, right?"

"Oh, the opening. Right. Was he fine?"

"He was, but that's not the point. He came with something new, something . . ."

"Talkin' about Kama Sutra or something? Some shit like that?"

"Naw, Kiz." Danni had to laugh a little. "It wasn't like that, had nothing to do with sex. He was on something different. I mean, talking my language, you know? I felt reconnected. I started remembering some of the stuff I used to dream about."

"A knight in a shining ride, coming to swoop us away from doing Ma's dishes all the time." Kizzy held up her glass for a toast. "Hell yeah. I remember that shit too."

Danni toasted her, took a sip, but said, "Not that."

"What? Doing the paint thing?"

"Seeing the world . . ."

"Oh, yeah. Right, right . . . How all you wanted to paint a picture someday of every place you ever visited."

"I hadn't thought about *any* of that in a long time, Kiz. And then, tonight, this brotha . . ." Danni sighed at the memories. "So *much* of what he said made me reminisce, think about some of that."

"Well, that's cool. So go. Do the damn thang."

"But then, before you know it, here comes N'Drea."

"Hatin'." Kizzy picked up the *Cosmo* and started flipping through it, stopping here and there at a pair of shoes she dug or a caption that made her laugh. "Look at this '50 Ways to Make a Man Moan.' Girl."

"N'Drea just thinks she's got me so pinned, like I'm so simple or something. Like she's conscious, and I'm not capable. First thing she says to him? 'Yeah, you know Danni's ex-boyfriend is a Piston.'"

"Girl, what's wrong with that? Fuck that bald-headed, jealous-ass ho."

"Just anything to make me look simple."

"You shoulda checked her."

"She thinks I'm incompetent. She just gave me that job because of Ma."

"All right look, otherwise, how'd it go?"

"The mayor came."

"With his sexy self."

"It was nice crowd. Hopefully, it did what we needed it to do. Spark a buzz, get people talking. I'm telling you, Kiz, this guy was awesome."

"Give him your number?"

Just then the phone rang, and Danni reached for the cordless. "I wish," she replied. "Hey," she answered the phone.

"What, no Caller ID?"

Danni took a deep breath, and cut Kizzy a look. "Dallas?"

Kizzy tossed the magazine back on the table and dared not move or breathe, a big I-knew-it grin on her face.

Dallas said, "I catch you at a bad time?"

"I, uh, no, I um, I'm not asleep." She got up from the table, looked over in the living room, back at the stones, the coffee she had yet to sip. She winked at Kizzy, "I'm kinda tied up right now, Dallas. I can't really talk."

"What, you got company?"

"Well, I—"

"Better yet, you feel like some?"

"No, Dallas, *no*."

Kizzy jumped out of her chair and whispered, *"What'd he say, what'd he say?"*

He said, "Come meet me for a drink."

"No."

He imitated her voice, "Dallas, *no* . . . It's only nine o'clock. What's up?"

"Oh, well," she replied with a laugh at his dead-on impression.

"Come see me." He mistook her laughing for an opportunity. "So I can handle that smile."

"No."

"Yes, gotdamnit," he laughed. "And leave that played-out no

back at the crib. At least say maybe for me, a'ight? I wanna talk."

"You sure have been drinking a lot lately."

"I'm chillin' tonight though. I'm just try'n to buy you a glass, say what I've gotta say. Come meet me."

"Ask me again," Danni told him, "and I'm hanging up on you."

"What'd he say, what'd he say?" Kizzy clapped her hands.

Dallas laughed. "A'ight. Come see me. Now. You bad, hang up."

"I'm trying to be polite here, Dallas."

"Naw, naw. Click on me. Come with it."

"First of all, I'm tired. I had a very busy day at work, a very momentous reception tonight. Dealing with people . . ."

Kizzy went berserk, started jumping up and down, waving her arms. *"Tell him about the fine-ass artist man. Tell him."*

"People better not be wildin' out on my baby," he said.

"Uh," Danni scurried into the living room, trying to get away from Kizzy's desperate antics before she cracked up laughing. "Actually, I met a really nice guy. An artist. It was, uh, very special."

"Special? What you mean *special*?"

"Nothing. Never mind. I've gotta go."

He wanted to know what she was doing right then, that very second, said he was laying low at Genteels, said to swing by, just for a minute, right now, just so he could say what he needed to say eye to eye, and he meant it. "A'ight?"

"No."

"What'd he say, what'd he say?"

Danni kept trying to turn her back to Kizzy, but every which way she turned, there was Kizzy, egging her on, whispering and carrying on.

"I can't."

"Why not?"

Kizzy hit her hand to her forehead. *"What, what, what?"*

"Because." Danni tried to turn away. "Because I—"

"Be here in the next half hour," Dallas said. "Or I bet I'll be over there. And you're not gone call the police if I do, so save it." He hung up.

She looked back at the stones, at the blank canvas, and she looked at Kizzy.

"He hung up."

"Girl *what* did he say? I swear that man still loves you, girl. He does."

"Please. He also loves French kissing, remember?"

Kizzy cracked up laughing and fell back on the couch. "So what'd he say?"

"Had the nerve to ask me to meet him for a drink. He *claims* that he really wants to tell me something in person."

"You are gonna go, right?"

"Please. Hell no."

"You should."

"Kiz."

"For real. Get yourself real fly, and *what*. Make his ass miss what he's been missing. I still say you need closure. That's probably what's got your flow clogged."

"Please. Let him see me fly so he can really start blowing up my phone. I'll end up having to get my damn number changed. I'm getting too old for games."

"Exactly. Which is why ya'll need to go ahead and handle this like adults. Sit down, have a heart to heart, know what I'm sayin'?"

"In an ideal world, that'd be great. But you don't know what it's like trying to get a straight answer out of Dallas. Plus, wasn't it you who called me today with the breaking news?"

"And? So use that. Girl, I'd give that man a good-bye kiss with so much current, get him all worked up and shit, and then just walk away. Look back and tell his ass I hope he's happy with the bonjour bitch. Watch *that* fuck him up."

"I can't even go there."

"You can't, or you *can't*? Because if you're feelin' it, girl, you need to just go on and get you some. Then tell his ass to get up and leave afterward."

"We're just different, Kiz. I can't do that."

"*Yes*, you can." Kizzy sat up. "For once, girl, just try it. Try doing what I'm telling you works. Thinking you're with someone else? Getting a good whiff of what he's gonna be missing? Oh, he'll come correct. You'll see. You think you can't do some of the shit I do, but you can. We're both the same."

No, they were not.

Danni and Kizzy were both twelve, the first time they met, and Danni was not happy about having to divide her room in half. But at least it was a girl, at least they were the same age. Maybe they'd have something in common. A few taps on the door let Danni know that Ma was ready to bring in her new sister. She looked up from the picture she'd been drawing, and in Kizzy walked.

Her clothes were unkempt, her white skirt not so white, and her legs were bony, her knees knobby, but she had the most fascinating curls that Danni had ever seen. She had a smile, so hopeful despite being abandoned by her parents, so bright and cheerful. She sat down next to Danni on the bed, and carefully, very carefully, she evenly divided the jelly bracelets she was wearing.

"Here." She gave Danni half the stack. "Now we can be twins."

There was such an optimism in Kizzy's eyes, something coming from somewhere way deep in the pit of her soul, an unmistakable hope. And there was also a clear hint of desperation. Danni agreed, even though she knew then that they were different, even more so now.

Danni flopped down on the couch next to Kizzy. "By the way, Ma called."

"Good for her." Kizzy cleared her throat and propped her feet up on the coffee table.

"She asked about you, said she wants you to come to church."

"Umm-hmm. So I can see the house *I* built. You know it's funny," Kizzy said. "You spent two years of your life with Dallas, and yeah he's been acting pretty fucked up lately, but then the minute he seems like he's trying to redeem himself, you refuse to hear him out. Ma, on the other hand, all she did, hoarding our money and shit, ain't showed no signs of remorse, probably never will, and you'll still talk to her."

"That's not fair, Kiz."

"But it's the truth. And you know it. You need to go get you some closure, girl. What could it hurt? Play it the way I told you and you'll come away with the upper hand."

. . .

Genteels was a pretentious cigar lounge downtown; it looked like a garage on the outside without even so much as a sign out front. Mostly, only card-carrying members knew about it and where it was, unless you were the guest of one.

Just to enter, just to sit down on one of those kingly-looking velvet couches, cost more per year than most people saved up for a down payment on a house, which did not include the price of one of those big fat foreign cigars.

It was ritzy, refined, and even smelled cozy. Danni had purposefully worn just a denim skirt and a red blouse. Though she'd kept on her red strap-ups, the only person she cared to dress to impress was herself. She looked around at all the other women in there, imitations of Playboy models. Then again, they might've actually been bunnies, for all Danni knew, for all she really cared.

Dallas was sitting by the far wall, a lacquer table the stage for a game of chess he was playing with some Suge Knight–looking brotha. Dallas was known to take a chess set to the club even, would set up a game in the VIP section, just so he could challenge himself, see how focused he could be amid the noise and the distractions, another method of practice before games. He looked up, saw Danni approaching, and said something to the guy, who turned, nodded a smile, and relocated to the bar.

"Well, well, well," he said when she was standing in front of him. "Danni Picasso has arrived." He tapped on the couch, the space beside him.

She surveyed the scene, wanted to assess her surroundings a little more. Was that Anita Baker, looking sharp and classy sitting at the neighboring table with her husband? When the woman smiled, Danni was sure that, in fact, it was, and she smiled back before sitting down across the table from Dallas.

A thick, diamond-encrusted platinum cross was hanging from his necklace. What a front. Please. Dallas might as well have been the devil in a fly-guy disguise.

"What up?"

"Hey," she replied.

He patted the couch again, and laughed. "What, scared you might get bit?"

She disregarded that, and looked down at the table, got a competitor's view of the game, and examined the black-marble- and brass-looking pieces on the transparent board.

"Bishop to queen," she suggested.

He repositioned himself, his leg touching hers underneath the table as he sat up. "Rusty. Look again, look again . . ."

She did, but saw no alternative. "As opposed to . . . ?"

His smile was proud, like he was revealing the secret to some fascinating magic trick. "Check out my knight, baby. Check 'em out, *right* now."

She considered this strategy.

"Oh," she said.

"Unh-huh. Checkmate. Feel me? Gotta be alert, baby."

"Not bad," she said.

"What you mean, *not bad? Sheeiiit.*"

She looked again, nodded a little. "Not bad at all."

"D. Laylock has skills, baby. Better ask somebody. Just like I got your ass out the house."

She thought about Roman Bilal, about the difference between skills and gifts, and she smiled. "Yeah, you've definitely got some skills," she said.

Dallas leaned in a little. "You got your chess players, and you got your muh-fuckin' chess *commanders,* know what I mean?"

Noticing the craftsmanship of the pieces, Danni bent in and hummed her compliments.

"Ah yeah, ya like that, don't you," he said.

"It's a nice set, definitely."

"You been playin'?"

"No."

"That's 'cause that new man of yours don't know how to play, huh? Buster."

"Please."

He leaned back against the couch. "You're lookin' gorgeous, as usual," he said.

"Thank you," she replied.

And just then, a waitress placed an empty glass in front of Danni. She looked up just in time to see the cork on a wine bottle pop. Dallas got out of his seat, took the bottle, and told the woman thanks.

"I'll pour it," he said, and began filling Danni's glass.

"That's enough," she told him a quarter of the way full.

"You sure?" He added just a bit more. "Your favorite."

She looked at the bottle, and it was. Franciscan cabernet sauvignon.

His hand was gentle against her hair as he gave it a lingering stroke, immediately dispatching an internal shiver throughout her.

"You said you needed to say something, Dallas," she said. "Never mind that it's taking you two months to say it, I want to hear what it is. Let's just get this over with. I need some finality tonight." Having said that, she took a sip of her wine.

Gerald Levert's "Baby Hold on to Me" began palpitating from the speakers, and Danni's heart started pumping like she was back at Perpetual Fitness, like she was back on the treadmill. But Danni remembered what Kizzy had suggested, and held her glass to her mouth again. The wine went down arid and forceful, but mellowed out real smooth in her chest.

"Come with it." He picked up a book of matches, and started rubbing the edges with his thumb.

"I think you're the one who should be doing the talking."

"What is it that you need to hear?"

"I don't know." She shrugged, rolled her eyes. "Maybe the truth."

"All right." He tapped the matches on the table a few times. "A man ain't got shit to lose but time. How about you ask the questions, and I'll give you the facts."

"Yeah, right."

"On the real. Go 'head, come wit' it." His eyes were penetrating.

"Okay." She put down her glass of wine. "Why?"

He looked perplexed. "Come again?"

"Dallas you had me, one hundred percent, ride or die like you said, and then you pulled the rug. So I leave you alone, give you the space you claimed to need, and then I don't hear from you for two months. And now all of a sudden you *won't* stop calling me. On top of that you question who *I'm* dealing with?"

"It's like this—"

But eff it. Too much was bottled up, needed to come out. Danni had only just begun. "And the nerve, especially when we both know that you're seeing someone else."

"Who?"

"That's right."

"Who?"

"So why not just let me be?"

"What you mean—"

"I gotta hear about you out with some French-talkin'—"

"French-talkin'." He laughed, knew just who she was talking about. "Man, I—"

"Please."

"What? You want the truth, I'm tryin' to—"

"It's hard for me to even sit here and look at you."

"I might've kicked it with her one, maybe two—"

"Dallas, stop it. You were just out with her. Just the other day, out at Fishbones."

"What, you got some damn paparazzo workin' for you and shit?"

Danni took a drink. "I don't even know why I asked. Not like you'll be a man about it, tell me the truth. Not like it matters."

He leaned back against the couch, whipped out his cell phone, and pushed it open. His jaws clenched, his thumb waiting to dial, he said, "I can call her right now, if that's what you want. She don't mean shit. I'll tell her that myself."

He pushed three numbers, a button at the top, and placed the phone on the table. Danni watched as the phone rang out loud.

He said, "I'll tell her right now . . ."

A forcefully feminine whisper interrupted the rings, *definitely* an accent. "You've reached the voice mail of Yonnis Campbell. After the tone, please leave a message. Have a blessed day."

Yonnis. Yonnis Campbell. So that was her name. Wow.

"Dallas," Danni said. "Hang that up. Nobody asked you to do all that."

He pushed the phone closed. "I'm ready to work this out between us, Danni."

"No, you're not."

"I am," he said. "I needed some space. Had that. Now I want my baby back."

"I can't deal with this." Danni pushed away from the table. His jaw muscles rippled. "Don't even try it."

"I've gotta go," she said, but didn't get up.

"Don't run from me."

"I'm not."

He tapped the chess set, no harm in his eyes. "A'ight then. One game," he said. "Before you go. Just for the helluvit."

"Please," she said.

But he still started resetting the pieces.

"I'm not in the mood for chess," she said.

"Scared? Naw, you bad, come on, beat me real quick." He finished setting up the board. "It's on you, baby."

Danni could hear Kizzy's voice, reminding her not to appear bitter, telling her that if nothing else she had to leave tonight with the upper hand. Danni looked down at the pieces. She put her well-manicured finger on a pawn, pushed it up two spaces, and sighed.

"You shouldn't say things you don't mean, Dallas."

"I say it, I mean it," he said. "Like what?"

"Like, how about until you're ready to be the man I need you to be, you don't mean things like that—you want your baby back."

"Well, I do. On the real. And what you mean, until I'm ready—"

"You figure it out," she said. "You think long and hard, long and hard, Dallas. We both know damn well you're not ready. Right now all that's on your mind is me being with someone else. One game," she recapped his request. "And I'm out."

• • •

The moon had settled into its position by the time Dallas walked Danni to her car, their steps slower than necessary. She glanced up at it, fat and milky white, and though she didn't consider herself to be superstitious, she knew damn well the caution a full moon evoked. She was definitely doing the right thing by leaving, pressing on with her life. Closure. Maybe now her creative doors would stay open. Maybe now Dallas would kill the offense.

"Get home safe," he told her.

"I will. And it was nice beating you," she teased.

He reached down to open her car door, but Danni had already reached for the handle, so their hands touched. He stepped in closer.

"You know I let you win, right?" His breath was on her forehead as his lips pressed in.

"Yeah, right," she replied, her voice unintentionally soft.

He kissed her forehead again, a tad longer this time.

"Dallas, I've really gotta go . . ."

He whispered, "Still not gon' tell me his name?"

She looked up at him, into his eyes. Could she do it? Could she lie?

"In other words," he finally broke the silence, "you're not gone tell me his name."

Her eyes dropped into a blink, and she kept them closed for a moment, just long enough to wash away the tears that she felt knowing that she was getting ready to drive off, that this might really be it.

"I've gotta go," she said again, opening her eyes and watching as he pulled his bottom lip in and bit down.

He stepped back and gave her a real good once over. He stopped at her open-toed sandals, saw her toes, and smiled.

"What?"

"My baby," he said.

She reached back for the handle.

But he stepped back in, pushed up against her, and his lips touched hers. And for some inexplicable reason Danni didn't feel the instinct to pull back, not even a little. She actually closed her eyes and felt the moment. Their good-bye peck.

She held out her fist, wanting to lighten the mood. "Give me some dap," she said.

He couldn't resist a smile. "See there. Come here." He pulled her in for a real tight hug, the scent of her perfume on his shirt now. He kissed her forehead again. "On the real, you know I'm gone miss your crazy ass, right?"

Danni could hear Kizzy's voice:

Girl, I'd give that man a good-bye kiss with so much current, get him all worked up and shit, and then just walk away. Look back and tell his ass I hope he's happy with the bonjour bitch.

Maybe it was the wine, maybe it was the moon, but Danni had gotten up the nerve to do just that.

He thought he was missing her now? Please.

She grabbed some of his shirt and pulled him in. And in that same moment, he reacted to their bodies being so close, to the desire he saw in her eyes. His breathing grew quiet.

She stroked the side of his neck with a soft grind of her fingernails. And then she kissed him, soft at first, and she waited until she felt him reciprocating before she went into fifth gear, before she led him on what she wanted to be a journey through the ultimate kiss of their relationship, of his life.

She wanted to give him a distinct reminder of what he would never have again. He sampled the wine from her tongue like it was water to his thirst, and she gave him more, and more, and more . . .

And then she stopped.

She climaxed her ploy with one final peck to his cheek, and let her hand relax on his chest for a moment. Once she could feel the thump of his heartbeats, she knew she'd won.

"FYI," she said. "I really do care about you."

He kinda laughed. "Now what? Just roll out on a man? Just leave me out here standin'? Got me all warm."

Danni loved the adrenaline rush from power that she felt. It galvanized her to tease him even more. "I'm not that type of girl, Dallas." She batted her eyes.

He jaw muscles rippled. "Type is that?"

"Sex without commitment."

"Trippin'."

"I'm serious. I've gotta go." She reached back for the handle.

"I hear what you sayin' . . ." He reached for her hand and held it. "But you feel it too, don't you?"

Because if you're feelin' it, girl, you need to just go on and get you some. Then tell his ass to get up and leave afterward.

Damn that Kizzy.

Was Danni really getting ready to play herself? Could she

handle this? It was one thing to hear Kizzy's voice, but it was another to *do* what she suggested, and then stay sane long enough to tell about it. Danni didn't want to get caught up again. Not like that. Make love to him, and then never see him again? Please.

But damn, it *had* been two months since she'd had this kind of affection. His breath was on her neck again, continuous soft touches from his lips.

Something had hit her inside like a big old ball of air, had been impossible to see coming. Now it was too late to brace for impact. Danni was hit.

"After tonight," she told herself, "it's a wrap."

She fumbled around in her purse for the spare key, and placed it in his palm.

Again he kissed her forehead. "Just need to cash out, get my set," he said. "Be through in a half hour."

She looked down at her watch. It was eleven-thirty.

. . .

His arms pulling her close awakened her, and her eyes reacted, fluttering at first. She looked over at her nightstand, strained to see the time, and her blinking went mad. It was almost one-thirty!

He kissed her neck and whispered, "Go back to sleep."

But Danni's eyes had rested long enough, now they were wide open. She snapped, "Did you just get here?"

His fingers crawled across her stomach, the black lace of her negligee, and he pulled her closer. "Sorry it took so lon" He had the nerve to apologize. "Go back to sleep."

Five. Four. Three. Two. One.

And then he was snoring.

She popped his arm. "Dallas!"

His snoring ceased. "What up?"

She pushed his arm off her and sat up. "Wake up."

"What? Damn."

In the dark she could make out his silhouette.

Nothing except boxer shorts on.

Too tired to even pull back the sheets?

She leaped out of bed, stormed into the kitchen.

He called after her, "Danni!"

"What," she snapped back.

"What's wrong with you?"

She snatched an aluminum pan out of the refrigerator and a few random pieces of rice and peas jumped onto the floor. She frowned at the visible brittleness of the rice, tossed the whole damn thing in the garbage can. Didn't bother to sweep. She pulled some Tupperware out of the refrigerator instead, started running the water, and poured in some Palmolive.

Just as she went back to the refrigerator to see what else needed to be cleaned, they met, face to face, in the doorway.

He had the audacity to look concerned. "You a'ight?"

"Kiss my ass and leave," she replied.

His lips curled up into that naughty grin. "Oh, I'll do the first part."

se shoved his chest. "Fuck you, and leave my key."

"Oh, so you really want me to leave?"

She reached in the sink, cupped a handful of scalding water, splashed it at him, but he jumped away in time and then managed to grab her wrists before she reached back into the sink.

"Danni." He squeezed her wrists. "Relax, baby."

She tried like a madwoman to pull away, but couldn't. Irritated, but too frustrated to keep trying, she chose not to bother. Eff it. Let him hold her. Eventually, he'd have to let go. "You jerk," she hissed.

He chuckled. "Danni."

And then she realized. What was she doing? This wasn't her man anymore. She had no say over how late he got in, over him taking too long to come over. She felt her entire body mellow, and she was glad to remember that she really didn't have a reason to be so upset. She sniffed, blinked away a tear that turned out to be unnecessary.

She softened her voice. "What happened to a half hour?"

"Man, Rock's girl had him locked out the house. I had to take him all the way to my crib—"

Yeah, right. Danni managed to snatch her arms away this time since he wasn't on guard, turned the water off, and shoved her way past him. But she noticed that look. *Might not getcha now . . .*

"Hold up," he called. "Hold up a minute, Danni. Damn. Shit."

She rumbled around for a pair of pajamas, preferably cotton and floor-length, and she remembered the day she'd bought that damn lingerie she was wearing, how she had watched as the saleslady prepared her perfect selection, a black lace number with delicate pearls up the side. It was a getup that hugged, sucked in, pushed up, and exposed her in all the right places. Something that brought out the spicy in her cinnamon-brown skin.

Danni had been so anxious, watching as that woman worked in meticulous movements, as she hand-wrote the receipt in calligraphy, the way she had tucked and folded Danni's selection with as much care and consideration as if it were going back on display. The way that woman had wondered aloud if it was for a special occasion.

Her purchase now blanketed by gold tissue paper, Danni had replied, "My two-year anniversary."

Dallas pressed his body up against hers, sedating her frustration with the cape of his arms.

She gripped one of her nightgowns. "This wasn't a good idea, Dallas. You should leave."

He whispered, "You really want me to go?"

"You told me thirty minutes," she reminded him.

"And I just *told* you what happened," he said quietly, kissed her neck.

"You could've called."

"I *did*. You didn't answer. Check your voice mail, while you're layin' up in here like a log, didn't even hear me come in." He groaned, kissed her neck. "Now let me hold you."

She was so angry that she could feel her heart beating inside her ears. "Just leave."

He nibbled on the side of her neck. "You really want me to go?" He lifted her hair up and kissed the back of her neck.

"And then you come in, fall right to sleep? Naw."

"I'm tired, baby."

"I'm not your baby anymore, Dallas."

"How about," he said, "we debate that under the sheets?"

"Dallas . . ."

"I brought the rest of your wine home. And," he said softly in her ear, "I'm gonna go pour us both a glass. And then I'm gonna give you your surprise."

She felt herself let go of the gown, and with his arms secure around her waist, she twisted around to look at him. "What surprise?"

Delight was in his eyes. "You want it?"

"What is it?"

"Naw," he grinned. "Not yet."

She reached up, touched the side of his face. "I don't need your gifts, Dallas."

"Well, I wanna give it to you. And don't you dare," he said, his eyes heavy, "even *think* about coverin' up that body with some damn hot-ass cotton."

She hoped he could see the quiet desire in her eyes. He did. Could've sworn she saw him blush. And Danni remembered how much she'd missed him, how long it'd been since she'd felt his body, so strong on top of hers, inside of her. Damn if she wasn't weak inside already.

He kissed her shoulder, soft at first, but then more ravenous. With his teeth, he pulled one spaghetti strap down off her shoulder. Wet kisses hungrily descended down her arm, diligent, persistent kisses, and Danni was grateful for the pleasant tingles suddenly bursting throughout her.

His voice was a whisper, "Be *right* back."

She nodded a quick nod, having no idea why she was shivering, as warm as it was.

She heard him rumbling around, first in the kitchen, and then in the living room, and she stood still in the dimness of the room as she listened and waited.

He returned with the bottle of wine, two glasses, and a tiny blue box in one hand, a book of matches in the other. He lit the candle on her nightstand, and now that she knew he could clearly see face, she really wanted to show him how she was feeling inside, but Danni was too nervous to smile.

He blew out and flicked the burned match into the wastebasket, and then gestured with his index finger. "Come here," he said.

He sat down on the bed, pulled her onto his lap, and held out the tiny blue box. With his thumb, he popped off the top. A pair of luminous ruby studs, her birthstone, was awaiting her smile.

"Since," he said, "I probably won't be the one you spend your birthday with."

She took the box in her hand and studied them more closely. "They're exquisite," she said.

He slipped his arm around her waist and pulled her in for a kiss. "Put 'em on," he said.

She removed the silver hoops she was wearing, tossed them

somewhere on the floor, and waited as he removed the studs from the box. Once she had them in her ears, she straddled his lap, closed her eyes and let her head fall back as he pushed her hair away from her face.

Soon his tongue tasted her neck, every lick starved for her flavor. Danni wrapped her arms around him and, feeling weak with desire now, she held on while enjoying every one of his licks, kisses, and soon playful bites.

He pulled her in to him and, in the same movement, slid his fingers through the straps of her negligee and pulled them down, exposing her attentive breasts.

She watched the expression on his face, so much craving in his eyes, and a whimper escaped from her mouth as one of his hands so tenderly touched, then his mouth covered "the girls," one at a time. Every suck felt so good that it ached.

"Dallas," she cried.

He stood up while still holding her, her legs still wrapped around his waist, her arms still around his neck, and he lay her down on the bed. With one swift move, he drove his hand up the center of her body and popped open every snap of her negligee. She ran her fingers through his mini-fro, pulled him close by his hair, and they kissed again. It felt too good to be wrong.

He rolled her over on her stomach, and pushed all that lace off onto the floor like he never wanted to see it again. "Baby," he said.

"Dallas," she cried again as she buried her face in the pillow and clenched hold of the sheets, anticipating, wanting, and needing every sensation that she felt. How was she ever going to get over him? Move on?

His mouth started at the small of her back, hard and deliberate as he kissed, and he licked and bit his way all the way up until he reached her neck, another quick bite before he kissed her ear, and then he whispered.

"A thorn, huh?"

Her heartbeats rippled and she gasped. "Dallas," she said and tightened her eyes closed.

He scooped his hand underneath her stomach, and turned her back over to face him. He came closer, pressed himself against her, grabbing hold of her knees as he did, but he waited a moment, abundant pleasure in his eyes.

With that naughty grin on his face, he said, "My 'L,' covered up by a thorn, huh?"

Danni closed her eyes, felt a new tear well up and fall, and then another. Both Dallas caught with a kiss.

A breath before they became one, he said, "The D is for what . . . ?"

"Dallas," she exhaled as he penetrated cautiously.

He kissed her shoulder. She stroked his neck.

"The L . . . ?"

"Laylock," she yelped with his first stroke.

"Where's the thorn, baby?"

Danni was too breathless to reply.

"Come on now," he said. "What's up on the thorn . . . ?"

"There . . ."

"There's what, baby . . . ? Come on now. I can't hear you."

"Is . . ."

He grabbed hold to her knees again, pushed *all* the way in, and stayed there for a moment. "Come on, now. What?"

"There is no thorn." She bit his neck, could hardly take it. "Shit."

Satisfaction in his voice, he groaned in her ear. "So you lied . . ."

"Dallas . . ."

"Talk to me . . ."

"Dallas . . ."

"Ain't gone *be* no muh-fuckin' thorn on my baby's back, now is it?"

"No."

After another real good push, he said again, *"Is it?"*

"No," she said a little bit louder.

He gave it to her hard, *real* hard this time. "Huh?"

"I said no . . ."

"Naw." He pulled out and rolled over, rested his hands behind his neck.

Danni gasped, felt an unimaginable void in her body, and she sat up, her breathing confused. "Dallas?" His body was like a canvas on an inspired morning, not enough, and how would she ever express all of the passion she felt?

"Come see me," he said. "Come say that shit like you mean it."

And she reached over, let her nails stroke from his navel to his neck, before she straddled him. With every thrust of her hips, she looked deeper into his eyes, and he into hers.

"No thorns." She tossed her head back, her hair now damp and heavier, and she promised him repeatedly. "No thorns . . ."

His hands, so powerful, grabbed hold of her waist and pushed up her back, and he pulled her in to him until their chests, both moistened with sweat, met to compare heartbeats, fast and resounding with passion now.

Their lovemaking was like taffy. Warm. Sticky. So good. Every one of their touches was more devoted than the one before, so sincere, so gentle. Danni wanted it to last for a long time, and it did.

The waxed flame on her nightstand eventually gave up on its own, and in the darkness Danni felt him push her hair off of her face, kiss her shoulder, and then there was the sound of him snoring again.

The final flicker left her alone in the darkness. It had been some enchanted evening, but Danni knew exactly how Cinderella must've felt, that damn poof lurking in the air.

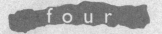

in the paint

A sharp sensation jolted Danni out of her sleep, and realizing that Dallas wasn't holding her, she reached for him. He was curled up with the pillow, far over on the other side of the bed. As had that flame, all remaining bliss had faded within her. Danni sat up straight.

Even his face was facing in the other direction.

Her voice was louder than she'd intended. "Dallas?"

His snoring was a soft, consistent tempo.

She was careful as she drew the sheet—white and soft like a lily's petal—over his back, the lingering moonlight offering a glimpse of what happens to a man's body after years of steady athletic training. Damn, he was cut. Danni pressed her body up against his back, and peered over. He started snoring even louder.

So, without a sound, she began sliding out from under the sheet. But when he stirred a bit, she waited until he'd gone back into that oblivious and satisfied sleep before she continued. It would have been ideal, to be in that off-planet place with him, but her heart felt too heavy to fly.

Her instincts felt the moisture in the air, foreshadowing rain. Might not be coming down yet, but Danni had weathered enough storms to sense another one coming. This had been a big mistake. Colossal.

Her foot unintentionally kicked the half-empty bottle of wine, but she managed to catch it before it spilled and woke him. Once he was snoring continually again, she felt around, was hoping to feel the long slim neck of a glass flute as her hand swept the hardwood, but she couldn't find it, so she took the whole bottle with her.

Danni's lips kissed the bottle. The wine, now hot and settled, burned down through her chest as she scavenged her brain for a clue to her restlessness. The only sounds came from the occasional dripping of water from the kitchen sink, and from Dallas's snoring.

Danni's thoughts raced like a flustered cyclone. She wanted to make noise, to drown out how loud her fears were becoming. She cleared her throat. *What* had she done? Was she really going to be able to say good-bye forever after a night like last? For her own sanity, she had to.

She took another swig. Panic suffocated her thoughts, every

breath bringing another pang, so Danni reached over and pulled the window open a little more, welcoming the wind. That enormous window was one of the things that she loved most about her downtown loft. If there was an event going on at the Fox, she could curl up and watch from above as folks stepped out of their shiny cars and paraded into the theater. Sometimes she just studied the bridge to Canada, massive lights leading the path to the popular clubs and casinos in Windsor. Tonight, though, it was all too much.

She felt around on the floor until she was able to slide her fingers into the belt loop of his jeans, and she dragged them into the bathroom.

For what she was looking, Danni really wasn't sure. She just wanted to, just needed to. The bathroom's halogen light was too bright, made her feel convicted, so she dimmed it.

Her movements were intentional whispers as she slid onto the edge of the bathtub. Careful not to knock any of the pumice stones off the edge, she settled into a safe position, and thumbed his black leather wallet. What could it possibly contain? Would there be a picture of Yonnis? A receipt from someplace they'd been?

Danni tossed the bottle up once more, was hoping to swallow courage in the process, and considered what Kizzy would've said. *If I get caught, I damn for sure better had done the crime.* So she opened it.

Driver's license. American Express. Visa. A few business cards. She peeked inside the billfold. A few crisp bills. A few receipts. She flipped through those. Gas station. Bookstore at the airport. He'd purchased a few magazines, an orange juice, and a pack of Big Red.

Still she resisted the don't-you-feel-silly impulse. Wrongdoing never jumped out and stuck its tongue out at anyone. She knew that for sure. Bullshit had a way of playing hide-and-seek. Always there, just had to be found.

She put his wallet back inside the rear pocket of his jeans, turned off the light, and dragged those pants right back into the bedroom.

Maybe she just needed to chill, relax, just enjoy the memory of a magical night. Mind over matter.

. . .

Thanks to the brink of day—Danni could see the few whiskers peeking out from Dallas's chin, and she remembered how she used to refresh his goatee. He absolutely loved it when she did that, sat on the sink, pulled him close, and pecked kisses on his chest between strokes of the Gillette.

No longer nighttime, but not quite morning yet, she kept watching him, and she found herself hoping for something to kill off her growing hope—perhaps Yonnis's name uttered in his sleep. But all he did was breathe.

All her life, Danni had felt like such a ragdoll, used, just wanting to be loved, and it was enough already. Lord, please.

She kissed Dallas's shoulder, and a definite optimism rooted somewhere within her whimpered again. Maybe he really did love her. Maybe this really could work.

But her mind resilenced her heart. Danni knew better than to betray her instincts with second-guessing. All they'd had was some bomb-ass sex, as usual. Tomorrow the stress would be back. All they had was last night. She'd give him a kiss when he woke, and say farewell.

Eventually, the room began to glow with the initial lightness of day, and Danni watched him wake with as much luminescence.

She stroked his chest, whispered, "Good morning."

His voice came out drained. "Umm," he said. "Tossin' and turnin' all night. You cool?"

She kissed his arm. "Sleep good?"

He yawned, a smile in his voice. "What you think?"

"I haven't slept."

He slid his arm around her, pulled her close. "What's wrong, baby?"

Baby. She laughed a little. "Nothing," she said. "I've got to be to work in an hour," she informed him.

"You a'ight? You gone be cool?"

It would've been nice to just lie in bed with him all morning, their hands interlocked, their voices exchanging reflections. But if she did, her phone probably would've just rang with constant questions from the office.

He reached over, cupped her breast in his hand, and yawned again before he leaned in and mischievously bit the side of her neck.

She lifted his hand up and let it fall on the bed, then sat up, pulled her hair back off of her face, and gathered the sheets to her body. Then she folded her arms across her chest.

A long stretch later, he sat up, too. With their backs resting up against the quilted headboard, they both looked straight ahead at their sluggish reflections in the contemporary mirror, both of them looking like they'd been on roller-coaster rides. "You cut your hair," he said.

"I needed a change," she replied.

And time ticked.

And ticked.

And ticked.

Each passing second brought more awkwardness.

She asked him, "So, now what?"

Both of their faces failed to hide uneasiness.

He looked solemn. She looked unnerved.

"Let's see what happens," he said.

Maintaining eye connection, she shrugged. "What's that supposed to mean? *See what happens?*"

He sounded so businesslike, so unlike him. "Maybe we just need to take things one day at—"

"Excuse me?"

He closed his eyes. "Can we talk about this later? I'm fuckin' tired."

"No."

Now his reflection turned to look at the real Danni. His voice shifted back to caring, more serious, less like he was half asleep. "Look at me," he said.

Only when she did, he couldn't stand it, the soreness that

reeked in her eyes. He looked down at her hand, now fisted and on guard. She looked down as well, realized it, but couldn't relax it.

He exhaled. "Forget what I said. I'm woke."

His hand massaged hers in a circular motion.

One final rub and she snatched hers away.

"You being happy, baby, that's everything to me. On everything."

"Just, whatever happens, happens?"

Her breathing grew heavier, more so with every breath. He eyed her hand, flat on the bed now, and reached for it.

She pulled away.

He had this look on his face, like he had the urge to hold her, but he didn't, wouldn't allow himself to, needed to say some things. "What, I'm back out here by myself again?"

"I need more than an occasional good time, Dallas, more than just good sex. I don't mean to make it sound like an ultimatum, but . . ."

He let out a long breath and watched the ceiling. So much aggravation in his voice, he said, "One-one thousand, two-one thousand, three, and I'm out the paint. Shit, the first gotdamn thing you learn when you step on the court. Ballin' 101, baby." More frustration this time, he said, "Feel me?"

Her leg rocked back and forth a little. "Do you hear *me* is the question, Dallas."

He looked down again, took his hand from hers and massaged his own forehead now.

She said, "You need to stop being so damn selfish all the—"

"SELFISH?"

"Yes."

He chuckled, couldn't believe that one. "Look at you, ear-lobes heavy and blazin' and shit. And I'm selfish?"

She reviewed another important fact with him. "Look. I like nice things, I do, and you *know* I do. But everything I went through with Ma, how I grew up *without,* you think I'm pressed to floss? I'm not. And you *know* this. I live on a budget, thank you very much, and I'm fine with that. Thanks for the earrings, Dallas, I do love them, but please."

"Yeah, a'ight."

"Do you want them back?"

"Man, I ain't sweatin' no change." He got out of bed then, pulled on his jeans.

She pushed the sheets off, kicked around on the floor for her slippers, and grabbed her robe. "I need to get ready for work."

He pulled his shirt over his chest, and, realizing that he really was about to leave, Danni's mind swelled with grief and regret. "Oh, my goodness." She slapped her forehead. "Why'd I do this?"

"Do what?"

She gave him a look, bored and unimpressed.

He grunted a laugh. "'Cause you needed to get served, baby."

"At least respect me enough to know that it's not all about sex with me."

"Ain't a relationship alive that don't need sex."

"I said *all about* sex. See this is why I didn't even——"

"Romance and finance. If you ain't got that, you ain't got shit but a friendship." He snatched his necklace from the dresser and put that on as well.

"Look. Let me just go take a shower, we'll talk when I get out."

"Screamin' my name. Scratchin' my back all up. Gon' try and act like sex don't mean shit. Meant somethin' last night, didn't it? All that you was moanin'."

She walked past him and shoved his chest. "Please."

He reacted with a grimace, hung his head a little. He laughed. "Always trippin'."

She snatched the bathroom door open. "I'm calm," she yelled. Then she forced her voice to sound relaxed. "And do *not* mention last night to me. Ever again. In life. In heaven or hell, wherever we meet again."

"Here you go."

The words had been on the tip of her tongue for weeks, months maybe, begging to be freed. "I wish I had never met you."

His knees bucked. But he played it off. "I know you don't mean that shit."

"My life has been nothing but fucked up dealin' with you."

"Oh, it's like that?"

"Okay, so we have good sex. Okay, so you can buy me the nice things that, yes, I like having. Okay. But what else do we have? Stress and worry. Wondering if this is ever gonna last. I'm tired of trying to pretend like I can handle this ride. I can't. You wanna see me happy? Leave."

He still looked like he wanted to reach out, to hold her, but he shrugged.

But she still needed to check another key point. "Point one. I never asked you for a thing," she reminded him. "Point two, all this baby-we-need-to-talk business, and you know damn well you're screwing somebody else?"

"Here we go again."

"Do you care about her? Do you love her?"

"Some ass every now and then, Danni, damn. Shit. That's it. You gotdamn right, *I said it*. There you go."

Danni's jaws clenched. "I wanna punch you."

He stepped his legs apart, planted his feet, and nodded up. "Do it," he said. And he looked like he really wanted her to. "Come on," he said. "Get it all out for once."

She lowered her voice, rolled her eyes. "Please," she said softly.

"So, we just gone end our thing over some female that don't mean shit to me?"

She shook her head. "So selfish."

He said sarcastically, "I'm selfish. Shit. Hell, yeah. I like *sex* gotdamnit. What the hell you want me to say?"

"Selfish. Selfish. Selfish. It always boils down to sex with you, doesn't it?"

He sat on the edge of the bed, his jeans still unbuttoned. Their exchange paused, but the room was not silent. His breathing was accompanied by the occasional clearing of her throat.

"This conversation is over," she said. "I need to get ready for work."

. . .

In the shower, Danni hoped that he would be gone when she got out. And, as she was drying off, she thought about how infuriated she was going to be if he wasn't. As she caressed her skin with cream, she wanted to curse out loud.

She had let her guard down, had lost sight of her mission, making sure that she was armored, always ready for conflict. That was her track record in battle. Every time she had felt safe enough to remove her protective vest, a bullet had seared through her chest.

Please. She came out of the bathroom with a don't-fuck-with-me look on her face, just in case.

He was lying back on the bed, his jeans zipped now, his shirt tucked in, and his hand balled up into a fist and resting on his forehead. He heard her come out, but did not sit up.

He said, "It ain't all about sex with me, Danni."

"Can't tell."

"Last night was that thang. Ain't nothin' like makin' love to my baby, but shit. I was happy just seein' you, just playin' chess like we used to do."

He sat up, inhaled, and looked at her.

"What," she snapped as she pulled on her black skirt.

"I tell you it's not about sex, and look at you. I tell you Yonnis don't mean shit to me, you still——"

"Please." She snatched her blouse off of the hanger and started buttoning it up. She was at a crossroads in the conversation. She could keep going straight, full knowing there was an emotional cliff up ahead, or she could turn right, tell him about himself using as many four-letter words as possible, let it all end on that sour note. Or she could turn left, cruise control, let things ride, make him have to realize on his own one day what he'd had, and have to live with that brutal regret. She did what she knew best to do, she busted that left.

"I need to get to work." She fumbled around in her closet until she found her black strap-ups. She sat down on the edge of the bed and lifted her leg.

He got up, a disconcerted look on his face mixed with sadness, and he reached down. He took the shoes out of her hand, and slid them onto her feet himself. With his jaw muscles tense and the room still, he laced up, first her left shoe, and then did the same for her right. Once finished, he stepped back, let her legs ease down and her feet touch the floor.

He stood there, a discernible uncertainty passing back and forth between them.

"Thank you," she finally said.

"You're welcome," he replied. "Sexy to me even putting your clothes *on* baby. You got it twisted."

"Please."

"A'ight. You want me leave, I'm out."

She looked away. "I never said I didn't love you, Dallas."

"So say it. Say it right now. Say you don't love me."

"Fine." She looked back at him. "I don't."

"It's cool," he said with a smile.

"My key . . ."

He tossed that tiny chunk of silver onto the bed, and she slid her hand along the warm white cotton and seized it. No more words were exchanged, neither of their lips moved to another word.

Watching him turn away, seeing his back to her, rekindled the bullet's heat, and it was Danni's instinct to hold her chest, to look away.

But she was still a soldier. As long as she still had breath, she could carry on. There was still hope. Love, she reminded herself, should not have to hurt like this. This pain, too, shall pass.

His footsteps faded down that long, narrow hallway, one deliberately quiet step at a time, and Danni flinched.

Cry today, she gave herself permission as she picked up the phone and dialed ReveNations. She was glad for the tears only because she had figured that, on N'Drea's voice mail, it probably really would sound like she was sick, like she really did have a touch of the flu. But, after this, she would never again shed another tear for another man. Ever.

• • •

By the time *The View* came on, Danni had prepared herself a scrumptious breakfast. Cherry crepes with cream icing, Canadian bacon, and with one push of that tool from *The Pampered Chef*, she had transformed a fresh melon into tiny chunks of stars. Now she was sitting up in bed in her satin robe, blowing at the coffee steaming out of her fancy porcelain cup. She could eat good, look good, and have a conversation with her own damn self.

The phone rang. She reached for the remote, turned down the volume, and leaned back against the headboard.

"Good morning." She frowned, anticipating yet another sorry-to-bother-you-while-you're-sick refrain from one of her coworkers.

"Is it really now?" Kizzy's voice blasted. "Umm, hmm. Tried you at work. You think you're slick. You sure as hell don't sound sick to me."

"Hey girl." Danni put the cup on the nightstand, and clicked off the power on her fiber-optic television. "I am. Mentally."

"What happened?"

"I fucked up."

"You went and had a drink with him?"

"I fucked up."

"How many?"

"Oh, I *really* fucked up."

Kizzy laughed. "Okay. Get your brag on." Kizzy was ecstatic. "Or is he lying right there, all crippled up and tongue-twisted after last night? Ya'll back in love?"

Danni crossed one leg over the other, both of them silky soft, and ran her hand down her hip, straightening out her robe. She let out a calm, cool, and collected sigh, and then a long-winded exasperated laugh.

"Damn," Kizzy said. "What's all that about?"

"I don't even know where to begin."

"Uh, hello . . . ? At the good part! Did ya'll do it, or what? How many times? In what rooms . . . ?"

"Once. All night. In the bedroom."

"Ooh, girl."

"And it was, let me tell you . . ."

"The bomb?"

"Atomic. Nuclear."

"Stop it!"

"Yes."

"Well, congratulations, then." Kizzy waited a moment. "Right?"

"Please."

"What?"

"It's still a wrap."

Kizzy screamed, "Bullshit."

"Ova."

"No."

"Yes."

"What happened?"

"I can't be in a relationship with him, nothing stable, not knowing when he's gonna do right . . . Nothing has changed."

Kizzy was silent.

"Kiz?"

"I'm listening."

"Yup. So there you go."

"Man."

"I'll be okay."

"I mean . . . What's the main thing, the bonjour—"

"Oh, he *claims* that that's just a sex thing."

"And it probably is. I'm *sure* it probably is."

"To me, sex is sacred, something you do with someone you love, *only* with someone you love."

"I heard that. But he's a man, Dan—"

"Don't take up for him, Kizzy. Don't do that. We're humans—different from animals. We can think in the abstract. We can make choices."

"Even still, sometimes we mess up, make the wrong choices. Like I said, he's a man. And not only is just a man, but he's a very *rich* man. Dallas Laylock, okay? What?"

"There's no difference between him and a *broke* man who needs to control his dick before trying to build a relationship."

"I know, but . . ."

"Kiz, please."

"Girl, when they said you didn't come in to work today, I said hell naw, my girl probably got proposed to last night. I got so excited."

"Not quite."

"That's all right. You're gonna have you a ring someday."

"He did give me some earrings though."

"Rocks?"

"Rubies."

"*Dayum.*"

And Kizzy was silent again.

"Kiz?"

"I'm sorry girl . . ."

"What?"

"*Babygirl.* Shit. Rubies? How big?"

"They're a decent size."

"Them babies are large, I already know."

"Okay, and?"

Kizzy sighed. "Girl, I am seriously pulling over off the street right now."

"Because?"

"Here we have this man, this very fine and very *rich* man, and the *first* night he gets some again, your ass is rockin' rubies."

"He said he had them for my birthday."

"Which isn't until July? Girl. Danni, my goodness. This man done went out shoppin' early for your ass?"

"Well, it's not like he can't afford them."

"No," Kizzy said with power. "Let me tell you something. *Just* because a man can afford shit does *not* mean he's willing to buy it."

"Correction." Danni switched into her we-interrupt-this-program-to-announce voice and said, "Guilt gift. *Hello?* Bonjour bitch." Danni slid down and fell back on the bed, rested her head on the pillow, and the slanted triangle ceiling looked hazy, so she closed her eyes. "The earrings are nice, but I want more. I want loyalty. I want . . ."

"No. No. No," Kizzy said. "Babygirl, come on. You need to call that man."

"Please." Danni felt her neck stiffen and her eyes grow warm, that pang in her chest. She would not allow herself to cry. She cleared her throat, dared not continue to try to talk.

"Dan," Kizzy said. "You all right, girl?"

"No." Danni's voice quivered. "I mean, I love him so much, but . . ."

"I know girl . . ."

"It's just so hard. All our lives has been so unstable. Don't you think it's time to flip it? Something real. Something solid?"

"Of course. But we're not talking about jewelry or appliances, shit. Men, relationships . . . Sometimes you just have to ride it while it lasts, move on when it's over."

"I agree," Danni said. "That's what I'm trying to do."

"Listen." Kizzy's voice was tender and relaxed for once. "I'll call Stacia right now, cancel my eleven-thirty facial, and be over there. Ben and Jerry's. A fifth of Hen. You tell me right what you want, whatever you want me to bring. I'm ten minutes—"

"I'm fine."

"Sure?"

"No."

"I know you're not."

"But I will be."

"Yes you will," Kizzy encouraged. "Aren't we always? Came into this world survivors. What? You're still beautiful. You're resilient. You're strong. No matter."

And then, for several moments Kizzy chose not to speak, just listened to the soft sniffles on the other end of the phone. Sometimes things between them didn't need to be said.

"Girl," Kizzy finally continued. "Everything is gonna be all right."

. . .

This time it was N'Drea's voice on the other end of the phone. "Sorry to interrupt," she said. "I know you're recuperating."

"Oh, that's okay," Danni said. "The TheraFlu is kicking in now." She finished fluffing out her pillows, gave each of them one last punch, and plopped on the bed.

"Ms. Blair, everything went exceptionally well yesterday evening, and I wanted to thank you, to express my sincere appreciation for a job well done. I know how hard you worked, how dedicated you've been."

Danni exhaled. "Well, thank you, N'Drea."

"Really. In all sincerity."

"I appreciate that."

N'Drea never just laid things on thick, never stopped with just four layers of icing, always had to make it ten.

"Danni, hands down, you are simply one of the most productive team members I could ever wish for. I'm sorry if I haven't said that enough."

"I'll probably come in early tomorrow morning to make up for today."

"No need to push yourself. Take good care. If you're sick, you're sick."

"I'm fine. That TheraFlu is a hot miracle, you know."

"Listen, just take care of yourself. Get your rest. We'll talk more later."

"Uh." Danni tried to think of something else to say, some

reason to keep N'Drea on the phone. Something felt weird, but Danni couldn't place it. "About Friday, the team *is* still going out, right?"

"Oh," N'Drea said, a diversion in her voice. "There's no need to concern yourself with Friday. Just take good care today. It's no big deal if you can't make it."

"Okay," Danni said.

No big deal? Since when?

• • •

Danni watched the scalding hot water fill the bathtub, the minted sea pearls exploding into bubbles, and smiled inside as she thought about something that Ma used to say.

My husband didn't know for sure whether or not I was a woman 'til the night of our honeymoon. Give a man free milk, he'll get used to not having to pay for it.

Danni sighed out loud as she turned the big silver knobs, inhaling the very last soothing second of water running. No more free milk. No more, no more, no more.

Next, she cued up a Chanté Moore CD, placed some fluffy towels and washcloths on the sink. A hot bath followed by an egg salad lunch, some pretzel nuggets, and sparkling cider, and afterward, Danni thought that maybe she'd watch a movie.

But after prepping the bathroom, she sat on the edge of the bathtub listening to the music, with this overcast feeling that she was forgetting to do something, like something just wasn't right. Ma had always told Danni to pray when she got that feeling.

She dialed the cordless and waited.

The answering machine answered. Ma's voice.

"You have just reached the Angel's Nest. Please leave a message after the beep. We'll call you back. God is good. Have a blessed day."

The beep didn't come. Instead there was a long high-pitched sound as someone picked up. Ruthless music blared in the background.

"Yeah," DeMarco's postpubescent voice shouted.

Danni smiled, remembering when DeMarco was but two years old, abandoned at the bus depot with a note pinned to the back of his shirt asking for somebody to take him in. Danni was fourteen years old at the time, used to read him Dr. Seuss books on the back porch. Always, he'd wanna turn the pages.

"Hey," Danni said. "What's going on?"

"Danni?"

She waited for him to turn the music down. "Yes." She put the receiver back closer to her ear. "It's me."

"What's goin' on? Unblock your number next time."

"Isn't it better to just not give your number out to people you don't want to call?"

"Uh." He laughed a little. "We're listed. Remember?"

Danni laughed, too. "Oh. Right. Where's Ma?"

"Where you think?"

Danni thought for a moment. "Oh."

"Yeah."

"Who's there with you?"

"Everybody. Rob, Melissa, and Jefferson are right here. Carrie, Pauline, and Tosha upstairs in the mirror tryin' to look pretty."

"For what?"

"'Cause they ugly. What you mean?"

"DeMarco."

"I don't know. Tryin' on some new makeup. Stupid girl stuff."

"Oh."

"So, uh, Kizzy dead or something?"

"What kind of question is that?"

"Ma said she ain't heard from her in a grip. Said she's gonna tell her about herself when she does call. She keeps makin' us pray for her."

"Kizz's fine. Still the same."

"Pauline's leavin' tomorrow."

"To go where?"

"Back to the zoo."

"DeMarco!"

"For real. Back home. Her mom's out of rehab."

"Oh."

"She keep cryin', actin' like she don't wanna go. Talkin' about running away and everything. Ma's tryin' to fight to keep her here. I don't know why. Always tryin' to run away from here, too."

"Are you serious?"

Ma had never mentioned that to Danni, never mentioned much to Danni unless it was a complaint about DeMarco, who for some reason Ma was hardest on, like he was the new Kizzy in the house. Danni always had to get the scoop about the other kids from him.

DeMarco's voice was muffled then, he said something to someone, and then someone said something back, but it was inaudible. Then he said to her, "We're playing some spades. That's about it."

Many nights Danni had also spent right in that basement, playing cards, but Uno had been their game of choice. They would stay up late playing that game, would end up falling asleep before Ma got in from church.

"Well," Danni said. "Just tell her I called?"

"I'll leave a note. I'll probably be 'sleep by then."

Danni knew all about it, how Ma would come in late, awaking the entire house with whatever gospel hymn she was singing, how she would stand at the bottom of the stairway and call out each of their names.

"Danni?"

And Danni would lift her head from the pillow, and call right back, "Check."

"Antoinette?"

"Check," Antoinette's voice would respond from the next room.

"Kizzy?"

Danni would pull the sheet over her mouth, make her voice sound a little higher, and call out on her behalf, "Check."

In the morning, Danni would rise earlier than anyone else, to let the dogs out back, to wave her hand out the door, to give Kizzy the signal so she could slip back into the house.

Danni held the phone, disarrayed, lost in the memories playing on grainy film in her mind, like a jumpy movie projector.

"Just," Danni told DeMarco, "make sure you guys lock up before you go to bed, okay? Call me if you need anything."

"For real?"

"Haven't I always told you that?"

"Anything?"

"What's up, DeMarco?"

"Aw, nothin'. Just askin'."

. . .

Danni had changed into a pair of fitted jean shorts and a tank top, and was taking a good look at that canvas, at the magnitude of its emptiness. Maybe she needed to get out of the house for a while. Maybe she needed some fresh air. Maybe she needed to exercise again.

Maybe she needed to go back in her bedroom, let her head hit the pillow, wait for Oprah to come on, and then the evening news, *Wheel of Fortune* . . . Then it'd be time to go back to sleep, back to work in the morning. Maybe she just needed to stick with the routine.

She wasn't even digging the idea of this stupid project anymore. A portrait washed ashore, off in the horizon. What had she been thinking? All she'd touched were the stones. Maybe it had been a whack idea to begin with.

Danni trekked into the kitchen, snatched a big heavy-duty green plastic garbage bag from up under the sink, and marched right back into the living room. Down on her hands and knees, she made swoop after swoop, and dropped the stones on top of one another inside the bag. And then she snatched the canvas, threw that in as well. She dragged that whole thing to the front closet, a deep crawl space in the back behind all her winter coats, and she stuffed it in, right back there with all the other paintings she'd pushed away.

A little girl on a swing, looking forlorn, her head down, unable to push herself, no one behind her to help. She never took quarters to the bank, but she, too, believed if she just had some gold . . .

Two little girls, exaggerated features, their arms linked together, dressed in some oversize Jackie Kennedy–style suits. She and Kizzy, back when they still had dreams. They were gonna make it. Someday. To somewhere.

Danni slammed the door. And locked it.

• • •

Sitting around moping was not an option. If she just kept moving, just didn't think about it, she'd be okay. She hadn't done Tae Bo in months.

Breakup sex. That's all it was. They'd had sex and broken up. All Danni had to do was fight the pain.

She leaned back, raised her leg, and readied herself to strike from the torso. Sweat was trickling down over her eyelids, blurring her vision, but she managed to look that Billy Blanks straight in his eyes when she bellowed out the words "Kiss my ass!"

But in her very next huff, she added a "Sorry Ma" out loud.

Ma used to fuss, would narrow her eyes as she cut her a long look across the top of her reading glasses, her lips pursed in disapproval of such language. She always used to say that Danni didn't have the tongue of a sanctified woman, talked instead like she'd been raised by a rebellious sailor, a foul-mouthed truck driver or something. Not much had changed since then, Danni thought, as she kicked out, yelled some more curse words at the screen.

"Come on now." Billy defied Danni's fatigue with his robotic-sounding bravado, beads of perspiration covering his face as well. He was staring right back at her. "Make it burn," he urged.

And she did. Burned right through her thighs like a bullet fresh out the barrel. She cursed some more, a lot more, and when she was finished she collapsed right onto the hardwood floor. Felt just like a waterbed.

She used the tip of her big toe to extinguish the power, zap Billy and the rest of his crew back into the land of too-fit-to-be-human beings. And she inhaled, took a hit of that feeling, the self-satisfaction of being able to—with just one single touch—make that bald-headed man vanish. Man, oh man, if only she had been able to do that with her desires for Dallas's body last night.

"Be gone," she commanded, just for the helluvit.

When her heaving calmed, and she was able to peel her throbbing back off the living-room floor, Danni looked up, grunted at the clock, wished she had just stayed cemented right there until her spandex was dry. Now what was she gonna do with the rest of the afternoon?

After getting dressed, she stared at her reflection in the mirror, still contemplating. She unloosed the bun in her hair and dialed her soul sister's cell phone.

"Hey."

Kizzy was out of breath. "Girl, what's up? Just leaving the spa—feeling *great*."

Danni finished applying her powder and slapped the compact closed. "You feel like hangin' out for a bit? I figured we could do Somerset, maybe hit J. Alexander's for lunch, my dime."

"Hangin'?" Kizzy laughed. "I'm sorry, I thought this was Danni. Who's this?"

"I'm serious." Danni lined her lips, and added a little gloss, hummed while she blotted. "I'm having a creative block ordained by the devil himself, and I don't feel like being at home. I need to unwind, have a little fun."

"*Whaaat? You* just used the words *need* and *fun* in the same sentence, girl."

"Please."

"Hold up. Talk to me."

"You wanna hang out or not? That's all I wanna know."

"Are you ignoring me?"

"Please. I am not thinking about Dallas right now. I told you, it's a wrap. I can go have lunch by myself, all right? Just forget that I called."

"Why so tight?"

"Nothing," Danni said. "All I did was call to see if you wanted to go to lunch. If you're busy, fine. Be busy."

"Look, girl, I know you're going through some shit, so I'm not gonna sweat how you're talking to me."

"Excuse me?"

"Danni, I don't want us to argue, girl. You're my sister, I love you, and I know you're tense. Let's just say whatever to this, all right?"

"Please."

Kizzy was brushing her teeth. Danni could hear her spit out the water. Then she said, "Danni, you know I'm always game to hang, but I have a lunch date already, girl. This fool I met at the—"

"Just say you have plans, Kizzy. If you can't go, just tell me. I don't need to hear about some fool you met, how much he's making a year, what kinda car he's driving, and where he has a summer home."

"Where's all that coming from?"

"You know what? I don't even feel like talking to you right now."

"Danni, you need to lighten up. I know Laylock—"

"Kiz." Danni rested her forehead in the palm of her hand, and closed her eyes, shaking her head repeatedly. Why did *everything* in her life feel so stressful these days? "Let me make this clear, like crystal, okay? Right now. Effective your very next breath, his name is forbidden from our conversation, and any conversation we *might* have in the future. Just like I try to be careful not to mention Ma to you, you can't mention what's-his-name to me. Got it?"

"Any conversation that we *might* have in the future—what's that all about?"

"Just forget I said it. Matter of fact, forget I called."

"I wouldn't be a friend if I wasn't honest, Danni."

"Go on. I'll talk to you later."

"Look. Where do you wanna meet? I'll cancel my lunch date. I need to grab me a few new pairs of shoes anyhow."

"I'm cool. Go on to your lunch."

Kizzy sighed. "We could meet at Somerset afterward, if you wanna do that."

"Enjoy your date, Kiz."

"You want me to come by afterward? I can."

"I'm cool."

"So, what are you about to do?"

"Nothing. Sit here. Reevaluate my life. Pick lint."

"I'll call him and cancel."

"Go."

"I'm trying to be here for you, Danni."

"I know. But maybe I'll just go visit Ma or something. Get out the house."

"I see! Like I said, you put up with her, but Dallas, a man who isn't perfect either, but really does love you, oh, you can't put up with him. All our lives, Ma kept ends from us, and you keep right on smilin' in her face, actin' like what she raised us just so right. She hurt you just like she did me, but did *you* ever tell her?"

"I'm over the money, all right? There's more to love—"

"Love? That woman didn't care shit about us but the fact that *our* money helped her afford to build *her* a new church. You call that love? Girl."

"She's all we had. She—"

"No. *We're* all we had, Danni. You and me. And you know it. What'd Ma ever do for us? Where was her ass every day all day? Church. Come on, now. Be real, girl."

"Stability. A home. She's not a perfect woman, but she took us in. She taught us how to pray, how to have a little faith in—"

"Let me put it to you like this, that woman's *name* makes me nauseous, like I just ate a bad piece of meat or something. She's a sick, evil woman, with one thing on her mind. Ends."

"Huh!" Danni laughed and the words flew from her mouth before she could reconsider. "So maybe *that's* where you get it from."

A numb silence lasted too long for comfort, so long that Danni thought that Kizz might've hung up. But she hadn't.

"You sayin' all I care about is money? You've got the nerve to say that? I never once heard you complain when Laylock kept your bank account swelled. Did you?"

"At least I'm changing. You're still chasing after a dream we had as kids, a prince on a horse, a castle in the hills. Still just wasting your life away. You snub your nose at regular guys, even if they're decent, just because of the kind of car they drive. Like you're so worthy. You act like printing out travel arrangements and saying 'have a nice vacation' all day is so fly. Like that's such a higher level."

"You know what? You can't hurt me. Say whatever you want. I'm me. I'm gonna have the good life. It's out there, and I want it. It's mine."

"Oh, but you're soooo different than Ma."

"You wanna sleep on Laylock? Go right on ahead. Just remember that there are a lot of other women out here who would love to pick up the pieces. And some of 'em speak French."

Danni pushed END on her cordless and then left it off the hook.

. . .

She had just finished removing those ruby studs from her ears, when her cell phone rang. She just knew it was Kizzy calling back to apologize. Instead, she heard a thunderous blast of music. She knew who it was as soon as she heard 50 Cent growl.

She yelled, "Hello?"

Someone was laughing, "What's up?"

"Turn that down, DeMarco."

He did. And then he said, "Sorry 'bout that."

"What's up?"

"Studying."

"Yeah, right," Danni said. "With all that noise?"

"My bad. Dang, what's wrong with you?"

"Nothing. Ma get back yet?"

"Naw."

"What's up?"

"You said call if I need anything."

Damn, why had Danni said that? She was stressed out enough as it was.

"What's going on," she forced herself to sound positive.

"Okay, if x equals c, right . . . ?"

"And what are you doing in summer school anyhow?"

"Because," he replied, "it's some old stupid stuff, man. My teacher don't like me, wanted my summer to be all jacked up, so she flunked me."

"So she's the one responsible for your grades?"

"Yup."

Danni rolled her eyes at his immaturity. "DeMarco, yes or no, were you having trouble in class?"

"Nope."

"So you understood the material?"

"Some of it."

"Did you ask her for help on the parts you didn't?"

"Nope."

"Why not?"

"Because. My teacher's a bum. Stupid. Man, I don't want no help from her. All she likes are the smart people."

"So get some help from someone else."

"Just forget it, man. You said call if I needed help."

"I'm just asking. They pay these teachers to teach, I just need to know why you don't feel like you can get help from them."

"I just told you. She's a bum. She hates me, she even lied to Ma, said I had a no-care attitude."

"Do you?"

"Man, naw."

"Okay." Danni grabbed her car keys and her purse. "So you're in summer school, why?"

"Man, I just told you. That teacher hates me, man."

"Okay, so do you think a tutor would help? Because you can't go to college if you don't graduate high school. You don't graduate high school if you don't pass this class."

"Not going."

She pulled on her leather Tretorns and laced them up. "You're not going?"

"Nope."

Even though he couldn't see her, Danni used her finger for emphasis, as if DeMarco were standing right in front of her. "Oh, yes you are."

He sang, "No-I'm-nooooot."

"Ma's not gonna take care of you the rest of your life. You turn eighteen, you're gonna be just like me, Kizzy, and everybody else. On your own. Then what are you gonna do?"

"Kizzy dropped out of college. Jeff didn't go."

"*And?*" Danni frowned. "I did, didn't I?"

"Kizzy gets to go to France, D.C., and stuff, man. Chicago, Egypt, Atlanta, Colorado . . ."

"You don't need to work for a travel agency to travel."

"Whatever, man. I'll probably be a Marine. Something like that."

"Fine, if that's what you want. Be a hero. But don't be a stupid one."

"Man, I'm just playing. I'm not trying to fight in nobody's war."

"So what *are* you gonna do?"

"Move to Detroit with you. Hook up with the rap game. I'm tired of Ypsilanti."

"So you wanna be a rapper now?"

"Producer."

"Yeah? That's cool." She locked her front door from out in the hallway. "But you know producers are basically engineers. Engineers know math."

"Whatever. P. Diddy didn't graduate from college."

"But he did go. I'm not saying it can't happen, DeMarco, but you stack odds against you when you aren't prepared. How are you gonna pay the bills, *eat,* in the meantime?"

"I don't know. Hustle. Shit on a pot. Clip flowers and sell 'em." He cracked up laughing.

"DeMarco."

"I'm just playin' . . ."

"No, you didn't . . ."

"Yes, I did." He laughed some more.

"I wish I could help you, but math isn't my thing, especially not algebra."

"Me neither. Man I hate math."

She told him, "Just be smart, DeMarco. Get help when you need it."

"I'm street smart."

Danni stepped onto the elevator and pushed the button for the lobby. "Yeah, you think."

"So, where's the man?"

"In his skin. He might be up on the moon for all I care."

"Oooh."

"So you just get on back to your homework, all right?"

"Ya'll get back together yet?"

Danni clenched her teeth. "Look at you, being nosy."

"Pauline said she seen ya'll on the Internet."

"Are you serious?"

"Nope. Tricked cha."

"Boy. You want me to call Ma on you?"

"No," he said real quick. "So she can have another reason to fuss? Man, I ain't on that."

"You know I wouldn't tell on you."

"Naw, I'll probably be a producer, but I wrote this rap. You wanna hear it?"

Danni was *not* in the mood to listen to DeMarco rap about girls, money, and the hood—three things that he knew absolutely nothing about. She mumbled her peace, "DeMarco, you better at least graduate high school. We'll talk about college later. Turn the music down. Get your homework done. Where is everyone?"

"Truth? Or story?"

Danni sighed. "Truth."

"Over some dude's house. I don't know. Picked 'em up in a big hooptie-looking car."

Danni put the key in her car door. "Tell Ma to call me, please?"

"If I'm up when she gets home," he said.

"DeMarco," she said, "I'm gonna call back later to make sure you finished your homework."

"All right . . ."

Sensing that he had something else to say, but was having a hard time getting it out, Danni sighed. "Anything else you wanna tell me?"

"I got basketball camp. Friday, Saturday, *and* Sunday."

"Basketball camp, after flunking algebra?"

"I passed all her other classes. I told you my teacher's a bum."

"Please. Enough with all that."

"But I *might* not go though."

"Why?"

"Because."

"Because *why,* DeMarco."

"Money was due last week."

"Did you pay yours?"

"Not really."

"Because?"

"Man, I told Ma, but something about the building fund or something."

Nothing had changed. Nothing. Nothing. Nothing. Ma was still pumping their money into the church, still acting like their monthly disbursements from the government was free money for Ma and Reverend Yandell's dreams, when it all should've been put aside for theirs. All that money she was pulling in from her congregation and she *still* was a mongrel for theirs? Please.

"How much is it, DeMarco?"

"Thirty dollars by deadline. Forty-five for late registration. It's late."

"Thirty damn dollars? That's it?" Most people tithed more than that in the first offering on Sunday mornings.

"Thirty damn dollars." He delighted in repeating her words verbatim. "That's it."

"I'll call the school tomorrow," Danni said. "I'll see if I can use my credit card over the phone."

He perked up quite a bit. "For real?"

"If they won't take that I'll just drive up and pay it in person. All you had to do was ask, DeMarco."

"Well, then, can I have forty-five dollars for basketball camp?"

Danni laughed. "Sure."

• • •

There was actually a guy working security at the back door? Oh my goodness. *And* he was flying high on a power trip. Ma must've thought moving up in the world put her closer to heaven.

He asked Danni, "Something I can help you with?"

Danni pulled off her designer shades, nodded at the giant metal door that led into that stadium-size house of worship, and said, "Here to see Evangelist Berry."

He gave her a suspicious look.

She added, "She knows me."

"They're in the middle of taping, but I'll see what I can do."

He held his walkie-talkie to his mouth, but first asked, "Your name?"

"Danni Blair." She opened her purse, preparing herself for his next question.

He spoke into the walkie-talkie. "Got a female out here. Here to see the boss. She says."

Female? Hadn't she just told him her name? Irked, Danni flashed her driver's license in front of his eyes.

"Blair," she said. "Miss Danni. I just told you she knows me."

He fingered the edge of her driver's license while he held the transceiver to his ear.

Static came through on the speaker, and a familiar voice spoke. "That would be her daughter," replied Reverend Yandell in his wobbly voice. "She's good."

The security guard looked Danni up and down as he spoke back, "Yes, sir."

Danni snatched back her license. "Thank you."

The novice security guard shook his head and smiled a little as he went over to unlock the door, and held it open.

"Sorry, ma'am," he said. "Just doing my job."

Sitting on a front bench in a first-class white suit with rhinestones across the lapel, a sharp white hat, and gloves to match was Ma. Someone was touching up her makeup.

Her laughter was simmering, and she reacted to seeing Danni. "Praise be." She smiled.

"Hey, Ma."

Seeing her looking so radiant, so classy, so elegant, and so happy to see her softened Danni's mood. Danni walked over, bent down, and gave her a kiss on her face, her fat cheeks tight and caked with foundation. Danni looked around at all the cameras, the spotlights on dim, a crew breaking for lunch.

"What's going on?"

"Come." Ma patted the seat next to her and asked the makeup lady to give them a few minutes. "We're filming the commercial," she informed Danni.

"Really?"

"You didn't see the security?"

"Commercial for what?"

"Just an invite to the community to come out and see us. We missed you on Sunday. How's my girl?"

"Kiz is fine."

"You see all this mess they put on my face? They say it's for the lights."

"Hmm." Danni looked around, up at the crystal chandeliers, and smiled. "I'm sure it is."

"What brings you all this way?"

Danni shrugged. "Nothing but a thirty-five, forty-five-minute drive," she replied. Danni wasn't sure how long it had taken to get there that day. She'd been too busy rehearsing what she was gonna say, words now she couldn't recall.

So she talked about the only other thing that she had allowed to be on her mind on the way over. "I'm really happy at my job, Ma."

Ma scratched her eyebrow with her thumbnail, and made a

face. "Well, praise be. I sure would like to wash this mess off my face. I know God didn't intend for my face to be itchin' like this."

Reverend Yandell approached, tall, slender, so aged now that he looked dead. He handed Danni a bowl of fruit. "Here, darlin'," he said, handing her a napkin as well.

"Well, thanks." Danni smiled. He nodded, told Ma they'd break for about ten more minutes, and then he walked away. Danni picked up a piece of pineapple, had to lick the juice that dripped down her hand. "Yeah, it's been going well. I'm really thankful for you helping me out like that."

Ma reached in, popped a grape in her mouth, her stuffed jaws pumping while she chewed. After she swallowed, she said, "Andrenita doing okay? She drove up here early in the morning yesterday. All this talk about funding for the gallery."

"Oh, really?" So *that's* where N'Drea had been early yesterday. "Well, we definitely need the funding."

Ma nodded in agreement. "That's what she was telling me."

"Hopefully we'll stay afloat until . . ."

"Hopefully so." Ma gave Danni a look as if there was no need to say anything more.

But there was more to say, so much more. Instead, Danni ate another piece of fruit.

Ma took another grape. "Have you been painting?"

Danni sucked on a piece of melon, shrugged. "Hardly."

"Oh . . . ?"

The whole way over there, Danni had kept hearing Kizzy say that Danni had never been honest with Ma. Well, especially after getting that call from DeMarco, now she wanted to be. She wanted to tell Ma exactly how she felt about the fact that DeMarco had had to call her and ask *her* to pay for his basketball camp.

But now, for some reason, Danni was on mute.

She flicked at the skin on a grape, watched the juice ooze out, and caught it before it ran down her hand. "I can't paint like I used to, Ma. I don't know what it is."

Ma reached over, picked up the grape, and rolled it between two of her fingers. "Uninspired? Better try God."

And then a hush brought another chunk of silence.

Now Danni was annoyed. Leave it to Ma to, off top, say something like that. Next she would just tell her how, if she came to church more often . . .

"You know," Ma said, "the word spirit is in the body of inspired."

It was a while before Danni answered. "I know, Ma . . ."

"You can't do it without God. Nohow. Not *nothin'*."

"I know, Ma . . ."

"Have you prayed about it?"

"No, Ma. I haven't."

"Oh." Ma chuckled. "Better get on them knees, girl."

Danni did the sensible thing, thought for a moment before she spoke, and in that millisecond she actually wondered if maybe she really did have the courage to bring it up. Not wanting to discuss what had been a constant burden in her life, and now the fallout between her and Kizzy, Danni clutched her purse.

"Well, you know, Danni, painting isn't much of a big moneymaker, is it? Every painting isn't sold you know."

"It's not about the money, Ma."

"Perhaps."

"You know," Danni bit off a chunk of kiwi, "Growing up, me and Kiz, that's all we dreamed about. Someday we were gonna be rich. Someday we weren't gonna have to worry about how we were gonna afford tennis shoes for gym class, hoping and praying we weren't in the same one so then we could meet in the bathroom and exchange the one pair we had. The pair we got from the Goodwill. Someday we were gonna have fancy cars. No more waiting on the DARTA in the rain."

Ma's body shifted, sat more erect, and she folded her hands in her lap. "Okay," she said. "I'm listening."

"So you go through life thinking, man, if I could just someday have me some bling to flash to the world, to sing out '*look everybody*—I finally got what I deserve, I'm worthy.'"

Ma chuckled again. "Okay . . ."

"And then you get that, but it doesn't really matter. Without it you're still the same inside. I don't care about the money, Ma, I never did. Sometimes, more than anything, you just wanna know that you matter, that you belong to someone."

No way was Danni going to end up some bitter woman, mad because she'd gotten cheated out of having things as a child. No. She was going to release all of this right here, right now. She angled her legs toward Ma, and their knees touched.

"Ma, when DeMarco called me today, needing money for basketball camp . . ."

"That boy is gonna worry me sick about payin' to go learn how to dribble a ball. Goes to school for free, ain't learning not a lesson there."

"Well." Danni swallowed. "Whatever the case, that bothered me. Especially when he told me how cheap it was."

"He needs to pass those classes *first*."

"I agree. But, Ma, Kizzy got real good grades in school. All she ever wanted to do was take dance lessons."

"That girl . . ."

"Ma we grew up penniless, but we were *not* broke. You kept all of our money from us. And you're doing it again."

Ma's face dissolved into a solemn expression that she modeled whenever her heart was heavy with the word. Danni's first instinct was guilt, but she disregarded that. No. She had a right to release this.

"Well, you know," Ma said, "that's a pretty big thing you're getting ready to suggest there—"

"The money isn't everything. You left us, all the time, in that house, by ourselves. Yes, our mothers and our fathers left us, but so did you, every single day." Danni set the bowl down on the bench. "That's the worst feeling in the world, Ma, not knowing if someone's ever coming back. You would think, all those years we would eventually stop worrying about hearing that key turn at night, hearing you come in. But I never stopped. Never."

Ma's body was stiff, like she wasn't sure what to do with herself. But then her face softened. "Praise be," she said. "God is good."

And Danni watched Ma's mind flip through a bunch of thoughts, comments, and scriptures. One by one, they were all defeated. What could she say?

She told Ma, "And you don't have to wonder if I'm thankful for all that you did for us. Our mothers gave birth to us, but you gave us life, Ma. I am, with all my heart, *thankful*. I'll always love you for that." Danni leaned in, gave Ma another kiss on her cheek, and took a good moment to remember how it felt.

Ma took another piece of pineapple, then another grape, her lips pursed together while she chewed. She looked down, a crack in her voice, "You, uh . . . you make sure you get home, get back in that paint, ya hear?"

"Hopefully, Ma," Danni said, "I will."

entrance exam

Her hair had unbunned itself, her blouse had worked its way out of the clutch of her skirt, and Danni hadn't eaten since two o'clock. One day off from work, and nothing had changed. It was after seven.

Danni yawned as she shut down her computer, and she noticed how quiet the building was. She didn't even hear N'Drea on the phone, at the copy machine, or her keyboard singing to a tempo even faster than Danni's.

"N'Drea?" Danni closed the door to her office and called down the hallway. "Still here?"

N'Drea's voice traveled from an around-the-corner office. "Still here."

It was almost eight o'clock.

"Need anything else?" Danni called back and held her breath. She didn't feel like doing another damn thing. She didn't really care about what needed to be faxed, sealed, or delivered, didn't care who hadn't done what when. It could wait. Would *have* to wait, whatever it was, until the morning at least. Please. She had every right to be a log on a couch after work, like everybody else. She sniffed under her arms. By now even her Secret was squealing the fact that it was time to go home.

N'Drea didn't answer.

"Hey." Danni stood in the doorway of N'Drea's mahogany-furnished office, manila folders and faxes carpeting the floor.

N'Drea was eating one of those Bugs Bunny–looking carrots and pointed it at Danni, "You can just knock those papers off the chair if you want. I'm sorry, I was so busy going over some things."

Danni maneuvered a path over to the chair, gathering a few papers here and there as she went, piling them together as she did. One of the letters was dated six months ago, should have been filed then. No way did N'Drea's office look like that normally.

Danni plopped the stack of papers on top of the window ledge, and then herself into the chair. "I'm so tired I feel delirious."

"You probably needed more time to rest. That stomach flu is a pickle."

Remembering the lie she'd told, Danni said, "I know . . ."

N'Drea crunched away at her snack, then motioned to her minifridge in the corner. "Carrot?"

"No. Thank you. I need some real food. Maybe I'll swing by and grab something on my way home, get something to go. Maybe some chicken lo mein."

"Ooh." N'Drea sank into her chair. "Now that sounds better than a carrot."

"I can call you in an order, too, if you'd like."

"I sure would like to say yes," N'Drea joked. "By all means, add a side order of deep-fried wings . . . umm."

"You have to eat, N'Drea. And it's not a problem if you need me to grab you something." Danni wasn't sure why she suggested it, as tired as she was, perhaps it was the strain in N'Drea's face, the way she looked how Danni felt.

"No." N'Drea swatted her hand in the air. "That's really very kind of you to offer."

"Sure?"

"I can't do rice. Pasta. Bread. Anything breaded. All the things that make life so much more sweet. I sure would like a loaf of Wonder bread though."

"Yeah." Danni laughed. "Well, man was not meant to live on carrots alone, N'Drea. Hey, if you want a piece of bread, as hard as you work, eat you a slice."

"To me, bread is like potato chips. The way I feel right now, there's no way I'd stop at one," N'Drea said.

Danni was thinking how cool it was, seeing N'Drea in her real-person mode, just kicking back discussing food, having what was borderline actual real girl talk. And then N'Drea spoiled it.

"I'll probably be here all night. Crunching. Crunching. Crunching. Numbers. Numbers. Numbers."

Danni noticed the calculator on N'Drea's desk, the open bankbooks, the stacks of envelopes, receipts falling out from a few.

"Is everything okay?" Danni asked.

N'Drea pushed away from her desk and took another bite of her carrot. "Well, Danni," she said, "actually, no."

Danni felt her face pale. "I'm listening."

"I was hoping to wait until after Saturday, to see how things go, maybe hear back from a few people. I wanted to know for sure that this would even be necessary. But you're so dedicated, such a team player, you deserve to know."

"Okay . . ."

N'Drea finished off her carrot, and tossed the end into the garbage can. "It's not good."

Tension was evident in Danni's voice now. "*It* being?"

"*It* being pretty serious. Revenue. Funding. No point in continuing to tap dance around it, severe financial distress."

"But the opening reception the other night, we had a house full. You said yourself that people were going on and on . . ."

"I know, Danni, I know." N'Drea closed her eyes, opened them a moment later, then looked at Danni. "It feels like a dream, saying this to you. A horror movie. One day things are just . . . There's so much hope, and then none."

"This economy sucks."

"Unfortunately."

"And I'm to the point where I'm beginning to *hate* money."

N'Drea reacted to that with hunched eyebrows.

"Really," Danni said.

"Well, I can't say that I hate it. I do hate the predicaments that the lack of it can put people in, however." She picked up a few folders. "For instance, today, three very pertinent phone calls were supposed to be returned to me," N'Drea rested her elbows on the desk, started massaging her temples. "Not one."

"May I ask from whom?"

"Saul Chapman."

President of Signature Bank. Danni nodded.

"Deborah Jenkins."

Founder and CEO of Urban International, one of Detroit's most influential African-American marketing firms. Danni nodded again.

"And," N'Drea said, "the mayor."

Danni felt uncomfortable as she realized that the common factor of every name that N'Drea had mentioned was that they were all key investors. In terms of life support for ReveNations, all three were oxygen tanks. The mayor usually always returned phone calls.

"N'Drea, you need to just keep calling. You know how you have to hound people sometimes, especially in the summertime. People go on vacation . . . and especially those people you mentioned. They're all so—"

N'Drea's smile was exhausted. "I agree. Trust me. I know what you're getting ready to suggest."

"You called them, repeatedly?"

"Of course."

"And?"

"I left very detailed, very distinct, very urgent, very clear messages. I wanted to ensure that every word I conveyed reiterated how time-sensitive my concerns were." For emphasis, N'Drea looked over and down at the phone on her desk. Danni's eyes followed. Not one red light was blinking.

Danni sighed. "Reverend Evelyn Berry. Not a dime from her?"

N'Drea shrugged. "Bad timing, she said."

Danni attempted to sound cheerful, though she definitely felt ashamed and embarrassed. As a favor to Ma, N'Drea had given Danni that job and *still* Ma hadn't a nickel to spare?

Danni said, "I've got the number to the mayor's assistant. I'll try her first thing in the morning, if need be. Before the day gets started, I'll at least make contact. And the others . . . We'll keep trying, N'Drea. Things are going to work out."

N'Drea was shaking her head back and forth. "Tried. Tried. Tried."

Danni took a breath. "Well, they've got the money. I mean, I can't imagine them just ignoring us forever, just never returning our phone calls. I mean, there's no way they'll tell us no, right? We've always gotten a yes before."

N'Drea got up from behind her desk, was still shaking her head as she came around to the front and sat on top of it.

"Danni, numbers are crunching across the city, the country.

A lot of creative bookkeeping is going on. People are trying to do whatever it takes to maintain. These are very frightening times we live in. Unfortunately, art just isn't a priority."

"I know," Danni said. She knew all too well.

"You're a smart woman. You're completely aware of the situation of the economy, the uncertainty we're all terrified of addressing."

"I knew things were shaky, N'Drea, but are they really *that* bad?"

"You know that saying about the big fat elephant in the living room that nobody is talking about?"

"Yes."

"Ours is magenta, wearing a polka-dot bikini."

"Whoa."

"We've got to talk about the elephant."

"This is awful, N'Drea."

"Reality. It isn't just for television."

"You've got that right."

"Some adjustments need to be made."

"Like?"

"So, anyhow, I've overlooked the fact that my phone calls haven't been returned. I know, when someone has to worry about keeping their own roof over their head, it's very difficult to call your neighbor just to say, I hope your head's not getting wet from the rain, especially when you know you haven't an umbrella to offer."

Danni was overwhelmed with dread every time she considered mentioning a brighter side on which to look, to help N'Drea to see. She knew she didn't sound convincing, knew it was corny, but she said, "We still have tomorrow, N'Drea."

"And the irony of that is that tomorrow will just bring more obstacles, more overhead to pay out. I'm actually dreading another sunrise. Time to face it. The other day I went over to Madeline Cooper's office."

"From the arts commission?"

"Exactly."

"I thought you weren't supposed to meet with her until the eighteenth?"

"Exactly. But I pestered her assistant, got her to squeeze me in on a less-chaotic-than-most day, and went for it."

"And?"

"Things aren't good for them either."

"Whoa."

"In fact, it's looking pretty damn bad."

"Okay." Danni sat up. "Have we forgotten about Tuesday? What other potential investors attended? Maybe we could contact some of them, see if—"

"Oh, they *attended*. Oh they ate, enjoyed the program, the art . . ."

"I'm getting a headache."

"It's down to plan D."

"We can come up with a monster marketing strategy. We'll get some more buzz going, we'll spark more interest. If I have to, I'll stand outside in a cardboard sandwich with some catchy slogan across the top, we'll get some investors to listen, to want to invest in the finest art gallery in the Midwest."

Danni was joking about the sandwich part. No way was she ever gonna go that far into desperation. All she had been hoping to do by saying that was to inspire a smile from N'Drea, at least a little one, just to confirm that optimism was still lingering somewhere inside of her, that losing her job wasn't going to be another bullet in her chest.

No, Danni had not been happy at work in a very long time, but this was still N'Drea. This was the same woman who had believed in Danni then, had given her a job based on Ma's recommendation alone, back when Danni was just starting out, back when everyone had told her we'll call you. ReveNations was Danni's only means.

"We've gotta hold on, N'Drea."

N'Drea did at least smile. "You know," she said, "that's the same fire that made me want to hire you in the first place, Danni. That sass. That self-assuredness. With you, it has always been this attitude of whatever I have to do, whatever it takes. That reminds me so much of myself."

Danni felt a *but* coming.

"Danni, you're an incredible woman, a consummate employee in terms of work ethic. And it is *because* you remind me so much of myself that I know you'll be okay." And then N'Drea was suddenly fascinated by the mini-blinds.

Now N'Drea was standing in front of the window, staring through the blinds, enthralled by the evening.

Danni was clenching her teeth. "N'Drea?"

"So many companies surrounding us"—N'Drea talked to the window—"and it's like, my God, if I could just somehow have one week's profit from just one of them, I'd have enough to bide more time."

Danni got up, marched right over to N'Drea feeling like she was Richard Simmons, hyper and ready to inspire. "So to hell with corporate dollars. What about the private sector? So we'll change the focus. All the entertainers with roots in Detroit, you mean to tell me we can't convince one of them to donate what they'd probably spend on nothing? Aretha Franklin. Smokey Robinson. Diana Ross. Berry Gordy . . ."

"You think they don't get people calling every day?"

"We could call WJLB, they help people all the time. Every single morning they're giving away something. We could have a fund-raiser. I'm quite sure for somebody, somewhere, a little help to us would be a very nice tax write-off for them. Some rich wife with her husband's checkbook is bored and needs to feel appreciated. Some accomplished someone, somewhere, wants to flaunt her money. I know it. We just need to put our heels to pavement."

Danni was not trying to be unemployed. Not today. Not ever.

"Danni." N'Drea closed the blinds and sat back down behind her desk. "I appreciate your optimism."

Appreciate? Danni had just offered to swallow all her pride in one big gulp, to not only just roll up, but flat out cut *off* her sleeves, go to bat like Derek Jeter for this woman!

"But," N'Drea said, "the important thing to always keep in mind is that there are no guarantees in life."

Everywhere she turned, no guarantees.

"Sometimes you have to adjust things." N'Drea pushed the cap off a pen, and started signing some random letter on her desk. Danni had to restrain herself from reaching across the desk, snatching it, and ripping it to confetti.

N'Drea was still looking down, though she had already finished signing the letter. She took a breath before she looked up, "ReveNations is looking at nine months to a year. Downsizing will be effective immediately."

"What?"

"I'm sorry, Danni."

"No."

"I know, I know . . ."

"N'Drea, the damn intern gets a stipend. You're telling me that you can still afford to feed her, to continue to pay her damn rent while she hasn't even finished college?"

"The intern gets two hundred and fifty dollars a week. No way is that going to keep the electricity on in this building, let alone pay the mortgage. If I thought it would, I would've done it."

"Companies cut from the bottom up, N'Drea. Not from the neck across."

"Sometimes."

"No," Danni disagreed. "You realize how expendable the new hires are, and you divvy their tedious responsibilities to people above them."

"Smart woman. You should run a gallery someday," N'Drea said halfheartedly.

"This is bullshit."

N'Drea laughed. "Call it what you want. I've considered bringing in a consultant, someone to assess exactly who is needed around here, but we can't really afford even that. I've even begun doing what I thought a consultant would do. It boils down to numbers."

Danni was wise enough to shut up now, to take as many breaths as possible before she prepared her rebuttal, before she got downright indignant.

N'Drea continued, "Yesterday, while you were home sick, when people did not have you here in the capacity that they've grown accustomed to, they actually had a hard time thinking on their own. I observed that."

"And you do realize that people called me all morning."

"I know they did."

"Question after question."

"I know it."

"Just *one*—"

"Let me finish, please."

"Fine. Please do."

"But also by the afternoon people called you less, am I correct?"

Danni considered that. "True," she said.

"Because they *had* to do it for themselves. Do you know what that means, Ms. Blair?"

Danni shrugged. "What?"

"If I were the consultant, observing this, who would I cut? All the people who need help doing their jobs, and have one employee left? Or the crutch?"

Danni sat still, in silence.

"The blurb didn't run in the events section, we needed to compensate for that. You weren't here, but it got handled."

"I don't know what happened with that, N'Drea. I—"

"It's okay."

"N'Drea, we talk for hours on end in meetings, and yet I still end up doing it all. Everything."

N'Drea eyed all the papers scattered throughout her office.

"Well," Danni added, "you know what I mean."

"I think," N'Drea winked her wink, "if we really took care to evaluate things, we both know that everyone is a key player around here."

There was a knot the size of a fist in Danni's throat now. She couldn't swallow, couldn't speak. Only a whimper of defeat escaped. TKO. Didn't even need the ref to count to ten, Danni had already left the ring.

"Danni, you show up and you're ready to work, every single day. Yet, of all of us, you're the only one who doesn't come out for bond nights."

"I've held down media attention, coordinated events . . ."

"Which will all look fantastic on your résumé. But, again, it goes back to the mission statement. Bond nights are just as important."

"Right."

"You're going to go on and do great things. I know it. You

can rest assured that if nothing else you will leave this gallery with a very commanding letter of recommendation." She handed Danni the letter she'd just signed.

Danni wanted to spit on it.

"I composed this yesterday," N'Drea said, "in your absence, a truly *felt* absence. It's the least I felt I could do."

Danni took the letter, but did not look at it.

As Danni stormed down the hallway, she was determined to make her heels verbalize her wrath. She pushed open the door to her office and kicked the garbage can on her way to find a box or something. Her pictures, her air purifier, the plant on her desk, all landed in the big black crate she'd found in a corner. Making sure that no one was standing in the doorway, she tossed her Rolodex in there as well. Let them power lunch and perky grin their own way to a fat black guidebook to powerful people.

Danni snatched the platinum nameplate from atop her desk. It had been a gift from bitch-ass Dallas, but so what? If he would've been there she'd have slapped him on top of N'Drea's desk, too, on her way out the door, out to freedom. Fuck Reve-Nations, fuck the so-called team.

· · ·

There was a night-owl, nine P.M. kickboxing class at Perpetual Fitness, and Danni made it there with ten minutes to spare. She just wanted to kick and punch, and to imagine faces as she did. N'Drea. Dallas. Ma. When she swiped her ID card, however, the girl at the desk stopped her.

"Uh, miss?"

Danni just looked at her.

Reacting to Danni's glare, the girl's smile was nervous. "Here." She handed Danni a padded envelope. "There's a memo on your account."

"What's this?" Danni was apprehensive especially now, noticing how animated the girl had been to give it to her, how eager she seemed to watch her open it.

Beaming, the girl declared, "O-mih-gawd, *he* was *so* nice."

Danni looked down, saw that her name had been written across the front in bold black marker, and asked, "Who?"

"He made me promise to give this to you, had to actually cross my heart and everything. He dropped that off last week."

A brand-new pair of black knee-wraps fell out from the envelope, right into Danni's palm. A note, autographed on the back of a Perpetual Fitness aerobics schedule, read, "Take care of those knees like you're taking care of that body, a'ight? D. Laylock."

Danni's mind swelled and her chest grew tight. It was just like him to be so thoughtful, sentimental enough to write down the date, and just like life to remind her that he'd also left that package for her a couple of nights before their good-bye sex, before she'd said she wished she'd never met him. Danni looked at the girl, not knowing what to say.

"O-mih-gawd," the girl said. "Isn't that cool?"

But Danni's throat was dry.

"O-mih-gawd," the girl said. "Are you all right?"

Immediately, Danni changed her mind about working out,

turned around, and left those wraps and that note right on the counter.

With a Kanye West beat to keep her energy up, Danni belted all the way up Southfield Road. When two beads of sweat trickled down the side of her face, she rolled all the windows down, let the night air in, and still pushed the air conditioning on.

She didn't even know where she was going.

She passed Claudia's Affair, the choice boutique where not too long ago she had purchased that black-lace getup to gift-wrap herself in. From now on, Danni would keep those hips, that barely-a-four-pack stomach, and her ample breasts in over-size T-shirts and boxer shorts, her hair in a bun. Big-girl panties.

Think, think, think. Mind over matter, mind over matter. Danni just needed to do something to release all of this adrenaline, to get back in touch again with whatever had kept her emotions in check before. She needed to feel how she'd felt the other night after Roman Bilal's speech.

She was stumbling, could *feel* herself weakening, but she would not fall. She would not.

. . .

The Office was a swanky jazz spot. On Thursday evening it was jam-packed with a very professional-looking after-work crowd, uppity-looking people nodding, snapping their fingers as some petite woman scatted at the microphone, drinking pretentious-looking concoctions, exchanging hurried remarks.

And sure enough, there he was. Danni spotted a seat at the bar and sat down.

His braided leather bracelet rested in front of her. And Danni looked up. Dressed in the bar's standard white shirt, red tie, and black pants, Roman looked like his mother had dressed him that day, like he couldn't wait to change out of those clothes. He looked bored at first, but then, recognizing her, he smiled.

He said, "A soda. No ice. Right?"

She strained to smile. "Kryptonite in a glass? If you've got it."

"Uh-oh," he said. "Not the same language you were talking the other night."

"Unfortunately," Danni replied.

"Sounds heavy," he said. "Kryptonite in a glass, coming right up."

Danni drummed her fingers on the edge of the bar, anything to entertain herself while she waited for her liquid relief.

She felt a hand at her waist, a voice close, too close.

"Garret Marshall," a tall, thick-glasses-wearing brotha introduced himself. "ExecTech Communications. National director. How are you this exquisite evening?"

Danni sighed, told him, "Not too good, thanks."

"I thought I'd take the initiative to come over and introduce myself. You're looking splendid."

He hadn't heard a word she'd said. Danni wanted to roll her eyes, but didn't, didn't even feel like the work it would take. She took the business card he had extended. "Thanks," she told him.

"My apologies," he said. "I didn't catch your name."

"Danni."

He eyed her hand, his business card still in it, and then an uneasy look covered his face.

"Oh," she said. "I'm sorry. I don't have any cards."

He nodded. "I see."

Then he just stood there, waiting for her spiel.

"Actually," she informed him. "I'm unemployed."

Garret Marshall, Mr. I'm-important-so-you-should-want-to-date-me, wanted to know if Danni was kidding.

"No," she replied. "I'm not just talking, hoping to get a laugh out of anyone tonight. If you wanna know the truth, I can really relate to the derangement of going postal right about now."

He told Danni, "You're like a comedian, right?"

"Garret. I know you don't know me, so just FYI, I take life a little more serious than to joke like that, about something as significant as my job, my livelihood, my bread, my butter, my mortgage, my car note, my profession, the things I put myself through college to acquire. I prefer not to kid about shit like that." Danni cleared her throat.

"Ma'am, I'm sorry," he said. "I . . ."

"And," Danni said, "I'm not looking to date. At all. I'm not giving up the digits, so don't ask. I'm not interested. And I'm celibate. And I might live the rest of my life saying that."

He had plastered a smile on his face, like Joker from the Batman movie. "Right . . ."

"Just," Danni said, "so you know. Right now. Off top."

Garret Marshall eyed his card again. If he could've done it without Danni seeing, surely he would have snatched it right back, ran away, pretended like he hadn't heard what she'd just said.

He played it off instead. "Well, you have my card. If you ever need freelance technical support."

A glass slid in front of Danni, and Roman leaned in. "Fella with the Coke bottles said for me to put this on his tab."

Danni's laugh was dry.

"But," Roman said, "I told him it was on the house."

Danni nodded a thank you, did a cheers with the glass.

He nodded his assurance. "My pleasure."

Danni looked at the glass after taking a sip. "This is Coke. Where's the Black Velvet? The Hen? The Long Island?"

He said, "You'd regret it later, reneging on your integrity. It's in the belly of stress when we must hold on to our convictions the tightest. That wasn't you talking."

Danni took a breath. He was right. So, so right. "Thank you," she said.

He said, "You're not sitting with the rest of the crew?" He gestured down at the other end of the bar, and Danni locked eyes with N'Drea across the room, who nearly choked on her olive. She swallowed, cleared her throat, laughed a fake-sounding laugh, and waved hello.

Danni looked over, saw, too, that Garvey was sitting two seats over at the very end of the bar, holding up a glass, and he pointed to it, then to Danni. He mouthed the words, *"On me."*

Yeah, right. He couldn't afford the bottom of the shelf Danni wanted to drink from tonight, let alone the top she was ready to order from.

"Oh," Danni remembered out loud, "bond night."

Danni swallowed some of her tenseness, and picked up her glass. Garvey was behind Danni now, his breath *reeking* of alcohol and cigarettes, and he kissed Danni on both of her cheeks.

"Hey, Garvey."

He whispered in her ear, "I've got to tell you about this woman I met. I'll call you."

"Okay." Danni laughed, full knowing that Garvey would have her in stitches as he recounted his latest episode. "You do that."

"Saw you flirting with that man a minute ago," he said.

Danni laughed some more. "So annoying. Thought that flashing his business card meant automatic access."

He finished what was left in his glass. "I didn't expect to see you here." He slid onto the bar stool next to Danni.

"I forgot about bond night. Otherwise I wouldn't be here."

"You also forgot to tell me good-bye."

Danni put her glass to her mouth and closed her eyes while she drank. She did the same thing two or three more times. "I'm not really down with good-byes, Garvey."

"We're actually getting ready to go," Garvey said. "Are you okay?"

"You know," Danni said to Garvey, "one thing that I know for sure, after all I've been through, is that not everything that hurts is bad, just as sure as not everything that feels good is right. Sometimes hurting, if it leads us to a better place, is a good thing."

"Yeah." Garvey definitely agreed. "And sometimes some people just deserve pain, deserve to feel fucked up. N'Drea's gonna get hers."

A twisted smile appeared on Danni's face. "Maybe," she said. "Or maybe not. Some people suffer. Some people don't." Danni twisted around in her seat a little.

Roman pushed the yellow receipt across the bar. "Here you go," he said. He was due to get off in about twenty minutes, said he'd be back, would join Danni and vibe for a minute once he was off.

Garvey saw the rest of the "team" preparing to leave, and, no longer allies, but never enemies, he and Danni shook hands. Again he kissed both of her cheeks. As far as Danni was concerned, ReveNations would just be one less battle to fight. Maybe someday she'd have a job where she didn't always have to feel the need to go over and beyond, always trying to prove her worth. She touched Garvey's arm, reminded him to call and tell her about his new love interest. But, with his eyes glossy and his balance a little off, Danni knew he'd probably forget.

· · ·

The place was dimmer now. It was a little after ten o'clock, and Roman Bilal and Danni were the only ones sitting at the bar, the only ones in the entire place practically. A table of four was engaged in a funny debate over in the candlelit corner.

There was the bald guy wiping down all the empty tables. And noise was coming from the back, where the owner was cashing out for the night. Otherwise only the slow tumble of her and Roman's voices filled the room, with an occasional clank from the kitchen.

He touched her arm. The chardonnay had helped her relax, not tense up whenever he did that, which he had done several times now. Already he'd mentioned his wife about fifteen dozen times, like he wanted to make sure Danni knew what was up. That was all good with her, too. Wasn't like she was here trying to snag a man. Please.

He told her, "So, that's what I mean. If I can look back one day and say, yeah, I meant something to some child, who grew up to be somebody, to know that I mentored a mind that mattered somehow, that made a contribution to society . . ."

"Right . . ." By now, Danni was tired of hearing about all he'd done for the community, all he hoped to accomplish. She was waiting for something, anything, to inspire her to put brush to canvas again. This brotha really needed to get high off his own supply, to take a sip before he delivered every now and then, to ease up on all this revolutionary shit. Damn. Let's talk about art. Get back to that. Make Danni feel like painting again.

He said, "You must be tired?"

"No," she said. "Why?"

"So much strain in your eyes."

Please. Life had waged war against Danni, and she was still breathing, wasn't she? So what if her eyes looked a little worn.

At least she was still walking the earth. "I'm not tired," she told him.

He accepted that, would question her no further about it. "So," he said. "I see all your key-chain-flashing coworkers were out in full force tonight."

"They can flash their way to purgatory for all I care."

He grabbed a handful of those Goldfish crackers. "I remember when my grandfather lost his job."

"How'd he handle it?"

"Took his severance. Opened a car-detailing shop. Let my brother run it when he got too old to deal with it. Things were cool 'til the U-Wash chain came in, took over the city. All the mom-and-pops shut down."

"I used to do that, have a blueprint for every aspect of my life. I used to set goals, do whatever it took to follow through on them. Now it's not worth it. I'm not gonna put all of me out there again, just to get pushed out, have to deal with a missing chunk out of my soul. Damn that. I'm just gonna coast for a change. *Que sera, sera.*"

He looked at her, something there, like he didn't believe her.

She put the glass to her mouth, remembered that it was empty, and put it back down.

"I've got all night," he said, still searching her face.

Danni had all night, too, but she was tired of talking, was craving some silence now, the taste of a spoonful of ice cream in her mouth. She also had an unopened gallon at home.

He was still watching her, concentration in his eyes.

Danni felt a flutter of annoyance that was mixed with a nervousness in the pit of her stomach. It was like he was seeing something that she couldn't.

"What," she said again.

"Something's wrong."

"Maybe I am kinda tired."

"No, you're not."

She felt her body strain to stay relaxed.

"You're in a struggle," he said. "Holding back."

"Please."

"And I'm intrigued." He pulled in his bottom lip, bit down on that tiny triangle of hair on his chin and then released. "You should sit in on one of my classes."

She perked up a bit. All this time talking, and *now* he was finally talking. "Where and when?"

"My place," he grabbed the napkin from under her glass, popped the pen out of his shirt pocket, and started writing. "Every night at midnight. Come tonight."

She raised an eyebrow. "Midnight?"

"Don't sweat the time," he said. "My wife and I are both nocturnal."

The drying blue ink showed her that he didn't live in the friendliest part of town.

She raised her other eyebrow.

"Don't believe the hype." He read her mind. "Nobody's gonna hurt you. If anything, they see an attractive sista like yourself roll up, they'll probably ask you where you're going, if you'd like them to walk you there. Thug soldiers."

He was married, for goodness sake. Wasn't like he was gonna try anything foul with her being there. Wasn't like she wasn't desperate for inspiration. Wasn't like he would hurt her. Would he?

. . .

Danni had every reason to be terrified. The neighborhood was eerie, the air thick with bitterness from having been raped by heroin in the sixties, crack soon after. Only the intricate details of the architecture stood as reminders of buildings once vibrant. Kwame Kilpatrick was spearheading an enormous renaissance of this great city, probably this particular neighborhood. No doubt, however, that Roman would pack up and leave once some cinema or TGI Friday's restaurant chain appeared.

The sky was a stale shade of gray, twenty minutes until midnight. Whispering men wearing hooded sweatshirts, their quick eyes darting up and down the streets. They guarded their turf at the helm of boarded-up storefronts, coughing up spits to the ground.

She stood erect, her head held high, her eyes nailed on the building two blocks up ahead. She zipped her pink Baby Phat jacket, her imaginary armor. Nobody could harm her, would dare try.

Under his breath, she heard a man say, "Hey now."

As she passed, another whistled his approval. "Damn, mama . . ."

This was their territory, she was from another part of

town—*that* part of town—might as well have been another country. And so it was only polite, respectful, to at least acknowledge the natives. So she looked at each of them, watched their eyes dance with lust.

She nodded, failed miserably at a smile. "Hello," she said. "How are you tonight?" She marched on.

Up ahead a little farther, a short and pudgy hand reached out in front of her, a silver dollar in his palm. "Watching you walk darlin', makes music play in my head. Sounds better than Ray Charles. Dollar for a dance?"

Danni did smile then. "Maybe some other time," she whispered. "Thanks anyhow."

One more block to go.

She heard a girl then. A teenager, it appeared to be, "Ooh, I like her shoes. Hey, lady, where you get them there shoes?"

Danni looked back, offered a smile. Wasn't it too late for her to be out? Wasn't she too young to wear high heels? "Saks," Danni replied. "Just a few months ago. I'm sure they probably have them in your size."

She nodded. Yeah, first thing in the morning, she looked like she was thinking, she was gonna have a pair. And then another look crossed her face. Not liking that expression, Danni looked away, hurried to keep moving.

She glanced down at the sidewalk, littered with broken glass, expired coupons, a dirty diaper, an empty cherry pie box from McDonald's.

Just a little bit farther. She picked up the pace.

And there she stood in front of his building, a quaint four-family walkup with a gigantic green door, brass knocker. She looked up at the stoop, the steps.

And then a forty-ounce bottle of beer slammed on the edge of the stoop so hard that she was surprised it hadn't shattered. She jerked, saw the man that had been drinking from it, and wished she hadn't. A lanky man, long arms and a braided beard, had a pissed-off expression on his face, in his eyes, and even in the tone of his voice.

He snapped, "What's wrong with you? Jumpin' around like that, like somebody's gonna hurt you."

Danni swallowed, prayed that she appeared calm, and replied, "I'm sorry. You startled me."

Her dainty sandals weren't ruby red and glistening, but damn if she wasn't ready to click them together, to start wishing she were back up inside her overpriced but highly secure downtown loft.

He grunted. "Ain't nobody gonna hurt you."

Danni put her foot on the first concrete step, the green paint chipped with age. She figured it'd be safer to find Roman than it would be to run back to her car alone.

But the man waved his hand in front of her. "Wait a damn second," he warned.

Danni took a step back. "Yes?"

He took a sip, wiped the fuzz from his upper lip. "This here is my building."

"I'm sorry?" Danni looked up, verified the address. Maybe he'd moved.

"I'm the access controller," he said. "Who you here to see?"

"Roman Bilal."

Hearing herself say that made her realize that she deserved to suffer the consequences. She barely even knew Roman.

He looked her up and down. He stroked the long skinny braid that was his beard and scowled, "He expecting you?"

She dug around in her purse. Where were her keys? What had she been thinking? "Uh, yes," she said.

"Uh-huh. You here for the class?"

Danni paused her searching. "Yes, I am."

"Well, I'll show you the way on upstairs. Not just anybody is getting inside this building, you know. I can look at you and tell you all right, good people." He started up the steps.

The building was dark, felt muggy and sweaty, the smell of thick incense coming from one apartment, burned popcorn from another. Loud jazz was coming from upstairs.

Inside the muggy building, at the top of the third flight, he stopped walking, held out his hand. His fingernails were filthy, a rubber band was around his wrist, and he had all kinds of visible proof of a man who had worked hard all his life, cuts and scars. Danni put her hand in his.

He jerked a handshake. "All right," he said. "The last apartment on the left is where you wanna be. You're a little early."

Danni looked down the hall, wanting to make good and sure. Yup. It was 3B.

"Thank you." She sighed.

He seemed uneasy, took another sip, and then he appeared confident again. He said, "Down on my luck. That's all. Don't mind my appearance."

"I see," Danni replied. "I'm sorry to hear that."

"Yeah. Roman's an all right man, you ask me, you ask anybody around here. I help him out from time to time, you know,
whenever I'm free, got some time on my hands. He looks out
for me. I need some squares, some hot juice, he'll slap me a
bill, two, if I need it. You get inside, make sure you check out
the wall unit, see the kinda work I do. You ever need something
put together, I'm real good with my hands."

No fancy business card, but promoting himself regardless.

"Okay." Danni was amused. "I'll definitely keep that in
mind."

. . .

Roman Bilal didn't answer the door. She did.

A tiny woman, wavy-wet hair in a stubby ponytail, she
looked biracial, like she was part Indian or Spanish or something, not even a hint of makeup on her face, didn't need it. Her
arm rested on the doorframe, identical rings on each of her fingers, thick silver bands, even on both of her thumbs. At least a
dozen thin, slinky silver bracelets adorned her arms as well.

Music, acoustic jazz, was coming from inside, and then
there was that alluring scent of warm apple pie. She wiped her
hands down her curve-hugging jeans, and Danni admired her
T-shirt, black with pink piano keys across the chest.

"Yes," she said, her smile welcoming. "Can I help you?"

Danni studied her some more, more closely. A pimple scar
above her left cheekbone. Lips dark from probably smoking too
much cess back in the day, or maybe today. And she was short,

probably five feet even. She was wearing Winnie the Pooh house shoes.

"I'm Danni," she said. "Here for the class."

She batted her eyes, but only once or twice. A nonchalant nod, and then, "Welcome." She extended her hand. "Sage." Her hand was warm and rugged.

"Thank you," Danni said.

"Rome's expecting you."

"Oh good."

"Some sista from the gallery, he told me. So much grief in her eyes. She'll come, he said. Told me to be sure and welcome you if you did. Funny too, I just finished a pie. You're welcome to some, if you're still here after it cools a bit."

"Okay," Danni said. "That sounds nice. Thanks."

"Come on in."

Painted right on the pea-green wall in the foyer was a mural of two God-like hands in shackles.

Sage said, "Rome paints the walls. He says he's never leaving this neighborhood. His roots, you know."

They turned the corner into the living room, and Danni was even more mesmerized by seeing that every wall, every possible available spot, was a display of more paintings without frames, coats of vibrant colors right on the wall. They were replicas, familiar imitations of slides from the seminar.

Sage told her, "Everything is his, of course. Except for that. That's mine." She pointed at a mahogany-and-brown quilt on the back of their green-plaid couch.

"It's beautiful," Danni told her.

"Have a seat," she said. "Iced tea? I could make pink lemonade, if my kids haven't used it all up."

"No, thanks." Danni noticed a stack of Polaroids on the oak coffee table. At the top of the pile was a close-up, the face of a teenage boy, dark-skinned, and with a closed-mouth grin.

Sage joined Danni on the couch and crossed her legs. She had kicked off her house shoes, and even all of her toes had thin silver rings around them.

"Is that your son?" Danni wanted to know.

"Spiritually," Sage replied, "he is." A gratified smile crossed her face, and she pressed her thumb on the white part of the stack of pictures, handed them all to Danni to look through.

"We started working on self-portraits this week. That's Christian," she pointed to the photo that Danni had moved to the top of the pile.

And then there was Tammy. And Juan. And Denny. And Robert. And Xavier. And Natasha, who preferred to be called Asha. Ten total. Sage seemed so proud of each of them. Her students were all her children in spirit, she explained. She and Roman hadn't started their own family yet.

"I see," Danni said.

"Art was the first thing to go with the big budget cuts, of course."

"I know."

"And ain't it funny? Money for sports, though."

Ain't it funny. Danni sighed.

"Sellin' our little soldiers the big hoop star dream, so they can grow up, get pimped by the industry, start believing the hype of fulfillment from big money, the illusion of sexual prowess."

Danni put the pictures back on the table, noticed a bookmarked copy of Fodor's travel guide to Israel.

Danni asked, "Sexual prowess?"

"You know how they do our men, pump them up to believe they're so much larger than life. And then they start believing it, start desensitizing their own sexuality, start behaving like savages, like animals acting on instinct, like they can't keep their dicks in their pants. Seek and conquer. King of the damn jungle of poonanny. Then they're all confused, 'cause they're chasing this impossible high, believing they're some kinda human Mufasa, when they're not. When they ain't never gonna be. They can fuck all day, ain't no sex gonna make them feel the power they think they got, that you get from spirituality."

"Hmmm . . ." Danni thought that was a bit much, but interesting nonetheless.

"No really. I mean, girlfriend, haven't you ever thought about it? The way they rape their own spirits? Who was that ball player, died a few years ago, said he'd slept with about ten thousand women?"

Danni was rubbing the bridge between her eyes now. "I, uh, I'm not sure."

"Yeah, well," Sage said. "I mean, me and Rome go to a game every now and then, so it ain't like we're not ball fans. But I can't stand it afterward. All those women lined up down the hallways leading to the locker rooms. All outside the parking lots waiting by the buses."

"So." Danni forced a subject change. "About the kids."

"Yeah, so we try to give them other dreams to consider. Not just hoops. Roman took the kids to hear Bob Johnson, what team is it he owns? I can't remember. But he gave a nice speech. Anyhow, so now that they can't get art in school anymore, some of my most promising art students, I let them come over for lessons."

"That's awesome."

"Ain't it though? And these kids, girl, they have so much talent, so much promise. And they're so hungry. You have never seen kids with so much hunger in your life, I'm telling you."

"Wow." Danni didn't know what else to say. Sexual prowess, huh?

"Uh-huh. You gotta see the makeshift studio that we converted the den into for the kids. Rome uses the garage for the adults. Asha, she does something with watercolors that scares me. It's just that incredible."

Danni nodded. She was thinking about Laylock, was wondering who he was with that very moment. She hadn't heard from him in days. It was really over this time. But she looked down at the picture, was thinking, too, that she'd like to meet Asha, some of the other kids. She thought about suggesting to N'Drea that they do a charitable art opening, let the kids come showcase their stuff. But she couldn't. Didn't work there anymore.

She thought about her and Kizzy, how when they were coming up they'd have loved to have known a woman like Sage.

Sage asked, "You have kids?"

Danni glanced back down at the Polaroids. "No, I don't."

Sage pulled a pack of Dorals out of her back pocket, said, "I know I need to quit, but I ain't gonna. Roman can go on somewhere with his speeches. One thing we all know for sure is that we gotta die. I'm writing my own death certificate. He knew when he married me that I'm a control freak."

Danni laughed.

Sage lit one up. "Why not?"

"Oh." Danni watched Sage take that first puff like she hadn't had one in weeks. "I'm not married yet. Haven't found the right guy, you know." Danni coughed away the smell.

"Child, I'm so sorry." Sage got up and turned on the fan. Then she crawled into the cloth recliner, curled herself up, sat there smoking away.

"My students are enough kids for me. I'd adopt them all, let 'em all live right here with me if they ever needed a place to stay though. I tell them that too, tell them that all the time. They're over here twenty-four-seven as it is. Might as well." she laughed.

Sage had done just what Roman had asked by kicking back, shooting the shit like that. Her vibe made Danni feel relaxed, like she, too, could kick off her shoes, pull her own legs up to her chest, stretch out right there on the couch if she wanted, that if she did, Sage would probably just ask her if she needed a pillow, a blanket, a scarf to tie up her hair.

Danni blinked away a tear. She could see why those kids were so crazy about Sage, why Roman spoke of her so often. She was the kind of woman who within five minutes of meeting her you felt like you could be yourself, that she wanted you to feel that way.

Sage's voice grew serious now. "Danni, I think it's so cool that you're a fan of Rome's work."

"He's amazing. A diamond in a sea of pearls."

Sage sat back. "Rome was right about you. I can sense it too." She made a big circular motion with her hand holding the cigarette. "Something's got ahold on your spirit."

Danni looked at her watch. Ten minutes to twelve. Would she be able to last that long without pouring out her soul to this woman?

Sage looked Danni in her eyes. "Who's your prince?"

Danni laughed through her verge of tears. "What prince?"

Sage sat up, put out her cigarette, and said, "He'll kill me for doing this, but let me show you some pictures." She hopped out of the chair and scurried into the kitchen. The CD ended, and now the apartment was quiet. Sage returned moments later, a thick brown photo album in her arms, an excited grin on her face. "I better hurry up," she said. "Before he gets back up here."

Sage was in every one of those pictures with Roman, looking pretty much the same as she did sitting right there, minimal makeup, jazzy-looking clothes. In one snapshot they were engaged in a deep kiss.

With that page on display, Sage said, "We've been together for so long. We go back like forever."

"How long?"

"Since I was nineteen."

"Really?"

"I know. And he's so good for me."

"I can imagine."

"But it ain't always been that way. You know that diamond you were talking about? How you think of Rome?"

"Uh, huh."

"Child, it took me a whole lot of foolin' around to appreciate that gem. Lucky for me, he hung in there."

Danni looked through a few more pages of fun-filled memories.

"'Cause when I was nineteen," Sage continued, "I was *fast*, you hear me? Girls Gone Wild ain't have nothing on me. Rome was the guy on the block, I swear he used to get on my *nerves*. Always preachin'. Always tryin' to enlighten somebody, especially me. Me? I saw the world as nothing but a big old playground to get kicks in. And Detroit was the world."

Sage took out another cigarette, lit it, and went to puffing on it again. "And it ain't been easy for Rome, let me say that, loving a woman like me is . . . But I'll tell you one thing."

Danni looked up from the book. "What's that?"

"Rome saw something in me, and held on, you hear me? You think I wanted to hear about the issues of our people? Child, I was strippin' at an after-hours, tryin' to make money for a new pair of Sassoons."

Sage took a long inhale, made one of those eerie-looking ghostlike puffs come out. "All these dogs, jerks, and creeps out here. Then you got a man like Rome. In tune with himself. Driven. Not afraid of commitment. Child, by the time I woke up to that, Rome wasn't a bit more thinkin' about me. I was nineteen and washed up."

Danni sat still. "But you still ended up together."

"I had to work like a madwoman, trying to get him to open up to me again. I'd have lost my mind if he wouldn't have finally given in to me. It took me going through a whole lot of jerks, a whole lot of sex with no meaning, to appreciate Rome. I wanted me a thugged-out cat, shootin' dice on the corner and thangs. I ain't want no commitment. Child . . . but you go through life with blinders on, you miss the paths you're supposed to take. Fortunately, I looked over at Rome before he passed me by. He tell you about Shahir? I know he did."

"Yeah," Danni remembered. "The guy who gave him the brushes?"

"My brother."

"You're kidding."

"He was." Sage's face looked sorrowful. Then she smiled a little, memories in her eyes. "Rome was Shahir's shadow. Shock, that's what we used to call my brother, saw something in Rome too."

"I love the way he took him under his wing like that."

"Yeah, I know," she said. "So, you know, if he wasn't at the center with Shock, he was always over at our house."

Then Sage jumped up, clapped her hands, and shouted, "Then, let me tell you, child! Whew! One day, seemed like I looked up, and a young *man* was knocking at the door, talking about he had some leaflets to drop off for Shock. Wasn't no kid anymore. All of a sudden his voice was all deep and stuff. I said, whoa-whoa-whoa, Roman Bilal done grew up on a sista!"

They both cracked up laughing.

Sage sat back down, put her cigarette out. "It was mutual," she added, a different, much harder, tone in her voice. "When it's true love, it is."

They listened for a while to just the sound of that fan, turning back and forth, blowing out warm air. Then Sage looked puzzled. She asked Danni if she had any brothers and sisters.

"Quite a few." Danni replied, thought about all the kids who had come through Ma's Angel's Nest over the years. Danni had never taken the time to count, but at best she had at least twenty-four siblings somewhere out there. Kizzy, though, was more than a sister, and Danni wanted to talk to her, wished that they'd never said the things they said.

"Where you from?"

"Here," Danni replied. "I guess."

Sage laughed. "From right here in the Motor, huh?" A vein appeared across her forehead. "You look Californian."

"What do you mean?"

"I don't know." Sage kinda laughed. "Like you had a privileged life or something. Like Posh ain't just a Spice Girl to you, like you know all about the finer things."

If she only knew.

Danni sat up straight, felt herself suiting back up. No more bullets. She told her, "Actually, I grew up in a home."

Sage didn't look as surprised, looked bored even. "Oh, really now?"

"Angel's Nest."

"Oh. So you're one of those girls, huh? Rich evangelist raising you. I read about her in *Essence*."

"It wasn't always that way. Used to be just a little blue house
Ma and Reverend Yandell bought, a place we all grew up in."

"What'd ya'll do, get Prada hand-me-downs from the neigh-
bors kids?"

Please.

"Yeah." Sage was perceptive enough to change the subject, to
leave Danni's past alone. "Rome and I have been together for a
long time. We had it rough for a while, but he graduated, started
getting gigs, and pulled us on through. Put me through school.
I definitely know what it's like to eat crackers for dinner."

Danni got a rush of her own memories, of her and Kizzy
making dinner for the younger kids, using Saltines for sandwich
bread on so many occasions.

"Me, too," Danni replied.

Sage laughed. "No I mean, for weeks."

Danni hesitated. But eff it. Let the truth be told, let this lead
to where it led. If she was gonna have to open up to truly feel
free, so be it.

"As a matter of fact," Danni said, "me, too. For weeks."

Sage reached for her lighter, her pack of cigarettes. "Don't
let me hold you," she said, a sparkle dancing in her eyes, a smile
growing. "Class should be starting. You can go on out back."

heat disclaimer

Roman pulled open the door to his garage/studio out back. Theirs was the last in a row of four.

Danni looked around at the night, the unfamiliar backyard. "Am I the only student?"

But Roman Bilal had already gone on into the garage, didn't hear what she said. "What was that?" he called.

And then, *clink,* he had found the string, had made the lightbulb in the center of the garage glow, made it possible for her to now see the inside of his small but impressive studio.

Cluttered with canvases, some unfinished, some brand-new.

All were abstract and strange at first glance. Peculiar, out-of-focus black-and-white photographs were on the floor.

He took a bottle of lotion off the table, rubbed a little into his hands. There was a mini-refrigerator on top of a card table, and he opened it, held one out. "Bottled water?"

"No. Thanks," Danni took her jacket off, sat down on an uncomfortable stool.

He went back over, started pulling the garage door down.

"Uh . . ." She flared her nostrils, reached for her jacket, stood up. "What are you doing?"

He pulled it down anyhow. "Mosquitoes."

"Yeah, well, don't lock it," she told him, watched to make sure he didn't, and sat back down.

He shrugged, looked like he didn't have a problem with that, like he really just didn't wanna get bit up by bugs.

He asked her, "Any trouble finding the house?"

"Not at all."

"You meet Vegas?"

"Who's that?"

He opened a bottle of water for himself and sat on the couch. "I told him to wait out front for you. Tall, frail-lookin' . . ."

"Oh," Danni said. "Right. The access controller. Yeah, I met him."

"Danni Blair," he stroked his chin. "Let me see, so you got your associate's . . . ?"

She nodded.

"Then you moved to New York."

She looked around, curious about so much, trying hard not to appear young, naïve, and eager to see. "Yeah," she said. "Came back to Detroit. Got hired, got fired from ReveNations. Now I'm here. In your studio. Waiting for class to begin."

"Well, all right . . ."

"Here I am."

"Here you are."

She sighed. "Waiting."

"Waiting."

"So is anyone else gonna show up or not?"

"Why so anxious?"

"I'm not."

"Twitching like you need a fix. You nervous?"

"I'd just really like to go ahead and get started."

He stretched his hand up, moved the hanging lightbulb, made it shine directly on her.

She had to look away, to protect her eyes. "Stop it."

His laugh was hearty. "Isn't that what they do to actresses? Put the spotlight on them?"

"To actresses, yes." She covered her eyes with her hand. "Would you quit it?"

He did. Danni felt the heat leave her face.

He made that ticking sound with his tongue, watched her face. "Why the pretend roll?" He plopped down on the seventies gold-leather couch, and said, "I thought you said you're an artist?"

"I am."

He stood completely still, so still that she wasn't even sure if his mouth moved when he said, "Trust whatever you feel. Be honest."

She looked away, shook off the weird and unexpected flutter in her gut. "What do you mean?"

"Danni, it's cool if you're curious. You want to open up to me," he said. "I can tell."

She took a breath. "I'm here for the class."

He said, "It's not like this is a test, Danni. Not like anyone else is here with us, gonna hear what you say. I'm not gonna tell anyone."

Only the sounds of crickets, a horn honking somewhere far off.

He didn't say anything. Waited.

"This is starting to feel weird," she said.

He shook his head. "Weird isn't a bad thing. All my life people have said I'm weird, treated me different, like a creature in the night for seeing the world different way. Because I'm not afraid. Tell me how you feel, Danni."

She hesitated. "What I can honestly say is that I've never listened to an artist speak, and felt so much, all at once, like the other night." A thought later she said, "It was almost like . . ."

"Like I was you," he said.

"But you don't even know me."

"I got Romare Bearden's spirit behind me, got Charles Alston, Hale Woodruff whispering to me. Telling me a little more here, a little less there. Alone, I'm just a man, like any other. I am a vessel, I allow things to come through me."

Danni wasn't sure why she felt the way she did, why he was looking at her that way, why she liked the way he was looking at her. She just knew that she felt close to feeling something. And that whatever that was made her feel nervous.

He fumbled around on the end table, picked up a black bag, unzipped it. Photography wasn't Danni's medium, but she recognized his camera as a classic.

"So what, you're a photographer too?"

He responded by looking out at the far wall. It was covered with dozens of framed black-and-white photos, various sizes—thumbnail, five-by-seven, poster size, and various tones—some grainy, some distorted, some straight-on.

She sat up, could probably look around that room all day if she had a choice, would constantly be able to find new things, inspiration increasing with every breath. She could probably explode in there if she stayed, if she continued to be pumped full of so many visions.

She hadn't noticed those pictures until now. Now she was preoccupied, fixated.

One was the inside of an empty coffee shop, a steaming cup of coffee was on a table, not a person in site, and smoke was in the air. *9/11* was the title underneath.

Another was of an elderly couple playing tennis on a run-down tennis court, laughing out loud, and in mid-motion. *Before Venus/Before Serena* was the title.

Moments captured with just one click. So honest.

He rubbed his camera case. "Do you mind?"

"Mind?"

Click-click. His camera captured her reaction. His voice was a whisper, "You're not camera-shy are you?"

Her body tensed without permission. "Not really. No."

He hummed.

Click-click. Click-click. Click-click.

Her head was so heavy now. She looked down. Hadn't meant to.

He said, "No . . . don't look down."

Her laugh was apprehensive, and she looked up. She found another interesting picture on the wall to focus on. Several pigeons surrounded a little girl whose face was sad, but not afraid. *Hungry* was the title.

"And," he said, "everything fell in place for you here? You got a job . . ."

Click.

He continued, "Fell in love . . ."

She looked down again. "I did."

He let his arm as well as the camera rest at his side, and he asked her, "And you've been together for how long?"

"We're not."

Click.

She lowered her head.

Click. Click.

She said, "I don't know . . ."

"You don't know what?"

Click. Click, click.

She didn't answer.

He asked her, "Do you paint what you see, what you feel, what you hear. Or what you want it to be?"

And then . . . *Click-click. Click-click.*

She was looking back at the couple playing tennis, when she felt his hand under her chin. It was gentle, the way he did it, but he forced her face to turn, to face him.

He asked her again, "How long were you together?"

She instinctively closed her eyes, affected but trying hard not to show it.

Click-click. Click-click.

And then his hand was gone.

She heard him fumble around, and then the sound of the zipper to his camera bag. She watched him put it away. He smiled, satisfied.

"I should go now." Feeling a little cool now, she shivered. "It's late."

"Trust me, you need this."

Maybe she wasn't ready. Maybe this was too much. Why, all of a sudden, was she consumed by thoughts of Dallas?

The first time they met. *To Danni with the smile. D. Laylock.* His cell phone digits were there as well. His arms. His tattoo. That naughty grin. The way she'd nearly broken her neck on the treadmill. The way he'd smiled when he saw her. The other night. The way they'd made love. The way it had felt so right. The way he refused to stop calling her baby. His voice. She missed his voice.

"Oh, yeah." Roman's voice was calling Danni back. "You need some release."

She focused back in and said, "You're pretty confident about reading my mind, aren't you?"

"What's your forte?"

"I told you, I paint."

"That's not what I was talking about. Breaking up. His choice? Or yours?"

She didn't answer.

He said, "You keep freezing up. Why the fear?"

She eyed his camera bag. "What are you gonna do with those?"

"Why the worry?"

"I have a right to ask."

"Does it matter? He's got power over you."

"Please. I don't see it."

"That's real power, when you can't. To be effective, power *has* to be invisible."

Danni felt too vulnerable, wanted to make him see how that shit felt. She put her hand on that black bag. "May I?"

He tilted his head, nodded. "For sure."

"So," she said. "How many years has it been, you and Sage?"

Click. Click.

"A long time."

"Are you happy?"

Click.

"Sometimes."

Click. Click. Click-click.

He said, "Mind if I ask you a personal question?"

"I'm asking the questions," she said. *Click.*

He asked anyhow, "Are you attracted to me?"

She looked over the lens. "Excuse me?"

He got up, put his hand on top of the camera. "Give this to me," he said. And he took it, put it back on the table.

"I love your work, Roman."

She felt his hand rest against the small of her back.

"Roman," she whispered, "you're married."

"Shhh."

"No," she pulled away.

He pulled her closer. "This man, the one who hurt you, did he cheat on you?"

She didn't answer.

He put his other hand around her waist. He pushed up against her and said, "I'm not asking you to do anything that you don't already wanna do."

But he *was* asking her to do something that she really didn't want to do. Danni really was only interested in his work.

"Sage is a beautiful woman, Roman."

"The world is full of nice people. Doesn't mean it's not fucked up."

"She trusts you."

"I trusted her too."

Danni reached back, lifted his hands off her. She sucked her teeth and narrowed her eyes. "So this is what men do, huh? We trust you to go off, do your thing, and the minute you leave, you've got your hands around another woman? Can't leave you alone two months and look at you."

Now he didn't answer. He picked the camera back up.

Click. Click, click.

"Please." She looked away.

"Look at the camera. Keep talking. Finally . . ."

"Please." She covered her face with her hand.

"What if I told you that Sage and I have been together for years. But we haven't been *together* in years."

"Please. That's none of my business."

"What if I told you she cheated on me, that I don't trust her anymore?"

"TMI. I don't care."

Click.

"What if I told you I was just in it for the kids?"

Click.

Danni looked up, right into the eye of the camera.

"You *don't* have any kids," she reminded him.

Click, click.

"What if I told you we fell out of love?"

Click.

Danni's face relaxed a bit. "But you are," she replied, realizing that none of the what-ifs were true.

"But what if I told you we're not," he said. "What if?"

Click, click.

"I'd say that I'm not interested in you, Roman. Not like that."

"Not even a kiss?" He laughed that loud laugh again.

Danni snatched the camera, fumbled with and banged on it until the film popped out, and she stuffed it in her purse.

His laugh was booming now.

She walked over toward the garage door, touched the rope to pull it open.

And then all of sudden he stopped laughing. "Wait," he said. "Why keep running? Why not face what's in you, what you need to release? That's the hardest thing sometimes to go up against. Yourself. Talent combined with fear is horrendous, has to be the most debilitating combination for an artist. For anyone."

Danni smelled cocoa butter, saw his hand on her shoulder. She turned. Heat was in his eyes.

"Class starts at one," he said. "Stay."

"I thought you said the first class was at midnight?"

"It was."

* * *

In walked the man from the stoop, the handyman who'd been her escort. He sat on the couch.

"Vegas," Roman reminded Danni.

Danni's back was uncomfortable, her butt still hadn't adjusted to the cold metal beneath her. Her hands were nervous, and her breathing tense. If she could just close her eyes for a few minutes, then maybe she could make all of it stop, the bursts of thoughts, the memories, the emotions, the longing. All that she feared, all that she'd been battling, had nothing to do with anyone else. Nothing to do with Dallas. Nothing to do with Ma. Nothing to do with N'Drea or Kiz. All to do with Danni.

Then someone else came in. He was in a uniform, but he wasn't there to fight a crime. A Bohemian-looking type, he was wearing an old policeman's shirt, something he'd probably gotten at the Salvation Army. He gave Roman some dap, looked at Danni and nodded, took a seat next to Vegas.

"And that's Po-Po," Roman said. He lifted the arm on an antique-looking record player, a few crackles later some Sly Stone song came on.

Another guy came in. Wearing a dingy bucket hat with the front rim flipped up, his stature intimidating. He looked like an aged gang member, in his forties now, still trying to be in charge. "Sorry, I'm late," he told Roman, pulled up a folding chair, sat down on it.

"What's wrong," he asked Danni. "You're not scared are you?"

"No," she replied. "You try to hurt me, I'll scream. Sage'll hear."

"Everyone in the building will. *But,*" he said, "you're not gonna scream."

Two more fellas and a chick walked in.

The dark pudgy girl said, "Dag, she look all scared. Like the bogeyman's about to get her." She laughed.

Danni frowned at her, frowned at all of them.

Please. She wasn't scared. She could handle this.

Roman said, "We're just waiting on one more person. Maybe he's running late."

She looked out the tiny window in the corner, down the alley. Across the street she could see an all-night diner, a now-vacant building where a sign still hung, MARVIN L. MILLER, ATTORNEY AT LAW. The light from the diner offered a glimpse into the depth of the alley. It was a short distance, but a mean darkness nonetheless.

He said to Danni, "I've got a blanket, if you're cold."

Danni looked over for the jacket she had brought with her. The chick, sitting on the arm of the couch, had it draped on her shoulders.

Yellow-stained eyes, the girl said, "Oh. I'm sorry. Is this yours?"

Danni didn't answer. She could keep it.

Roman's hand was warm, firm, and back on her shoulder again. "You have to be open," he said. "If you want change."

Danni felt a shiver, held her hand out for the blanket.

"I think we'll go ahead and begin," he said. He walked over, pulled the garage door down. Then he came back, reached above her, pulled the chain. Darkness.

And then a lantern on the table relit the room, gave a fire effect.

He picked up a pile of sketch pads, passed them out one by one to everyone in the room, except for Danni.

"Danni," he said, "just feel the rhythm of creativity."

She didn't respond, just enjoyed the warm blanket, agreed with a softly spoken okay.

"Good evening, scholars," Roman began. "I'd like you to welcome our guest. 'Tough Girl' we'll call her. Real name is Danni."

"Whooooo-weeeee," Vegas exclaimed. "That's funny. Tough Girl, eh?"

Said the girl, "She don't look so tough."

The two sitting next to Vegas on the cushionless couch just watched, anticipating eyes, clutching their sketch pads.

Danni's heart crashed as she felt Po-Po's arm on her shoulder.

"Glad you could make it out," he said.

"Danni," Roman said. "We'd like to thank you for joining us."

Her eyes scanned the room. Everyone just looked at her. All she heard was loud beating. Her heart.

A knock on the door. Another guy. The one with the silver dollar, had asked her to dance, came in. He smiled when their eyes met. He looked too nice to hurt her now, like a grandfather or something.

Danni pushed up the sleeves on her blouse, and realizing that she had balled up her fists, she took a deep breath and forced herself to relax.

Roman walked over to the couch, reached behind it, and retrieved a handful of lead pencils. One by one they took one. All but Danni.

"Danni, just relax," he said. "Enjoy the experience."

Her thoughts clouded in confusion. Maybe this wasn't happening. Maybe she was still waiting for the alarm to go off. Maybe it had all just been a nightmare. She was still dreaming. She hadn't gotten fired. Dallas was lying next to her, his arm around her waist. Or maybe that's just what, way deep inside, she wished.

The chick, now sitting with her legs crossed, said, "So what we working on tonight?"

"Fear," Roman replied.

"Cool," the one with the big gut replied.

Roman went over to the fridge.

"No, thank you," Danni said to the bottle of water he had in front of her face, her teeth chattering again.

"If you get thirsty," he said. "Let me know. Most of them are first-year students. This might take a while."

It was apparent from the beginning, from the first pencil she saw touch a pad, the big guy on the folding chair, that these students were serious about their work.

They'd draw for a while, Roman circling the room, humming along to Sly Stone, his arms tucked under his pits, nodding at some of what he saw, pointing this and that out. They'd take a break if they needed one.

Roman was like Robin Hood, had robbed every high-class art institution across the country, the world, every lesson he could gather, so he could return to his hood, to teach, to share, to inspire.

On college campuses all across the world, this very thing was happening, only the students were paying thousands of dollars. And he didn't charge his students a dime. One got up, grabbed a brew from the fridge. And Danni thought, *even the drinks are on him.*

They had no one else to teach them, needed someone who cared enough to reach back, to put a pencil in a hand, a brush. He was another Shahir, Shock as Sage had called him.

One by one, the artists started to speak. Blackjack was a blue-collar brotha, turned full-time hustler, turned con, turned man with a whole lotta regrets. Said in prison he started drawing, was hoping to master his craft now, sell some shit one day. He was exactly who Ma had been talking about when she'd said "an idle mind is the devil's workshop." He was witty, and sharp, but had never put it to good use.

Barten said he liked to get drunk most of the time. Used to be a bartender, hence the nickname. Said he remembered sipping a leftover glass one night. Few days later he heard himself telling someone about damnation and repenting, said then he felt confused, had no idea why he had been shouting so loud. Never went back to his job. Been fucked up ever since.

Susan was a shampoo girl, was hoping to someday be able to create those fancy hairdos she'd seen in *Vibe* magazine, go to hair shows or something. A seventh-grade dropout, she was twenty-four years old. Said she was saving up to buy a car someday, too. A Saturn or something.

Vegas said they called him that 'cause he was always winning the lottery. Said he used to build houses with Habitat for Humanity years ago. Then one day he just started having flashbacks from the war, didn't know why all of a sudden, he never had before. Said art was therapeutic for him.

There was Darnell, a seventeen-year-old boy who said he would sneak out after doing dishes, meet Susan on the corner, come to class three nights a week. Darnell was a pitcher on his high-school baseball team.

It was a state of unconsciousness that Danni found herself in. A trance. A daze. She stopped feeling, could just kinda see herself going through the motions, nodding her head, saying *oh really* every now and then. She was talking, but unlike those around her, she didn't have much to say.

Feeling her tension ease, Danni finally introduced herself. "I'm Danni," she said. "I don't know where I'm from, just where I grew up. I know that the scariest thing in the world to me is love. I'm afraid of losing. Anything."

"She doesn't look so scared now," Susan said.

Roman came back over to her, put his hand on her shoulder, that cocoa-butter smell still powerful, and nodded his agreement.

• • •

Danni pushed her hands down through the center of all of her hanging coats and spread them apart with one good push. Lying there against the back wall was her big black portfolio.

She would have to take a silk rag, wipe away all the dust, and use lotion to shine up that black leather case, but she would put it to use again. She pulled out the big green plastic garbage bag, too. First she would finish painting the stones.

Actually, first, she needed to do something else.

The hardwood floor was merciless on her knees, but that was okay. Danni folded her hands, rested her forearms on the arm of the couch, and bowed her head. *Dear God. It's been a while since I've prayed, and I am ashamed. A long time ago Ma told me that if ever something didn't feel right, if ever I felt a weight in my heart, I should fall on my knees, but I was not obedient. Instead I exercised. In-*

stead I worked long hours. Instead I closed out the world, blamed others for my pain and frustration. Ma always told me to count my blessings. I haven't done that enough. I'm thankful for Roman Bilal, for his wife, Sage. I'm thankful for Kizzy. I'm thankful for my talent. And also, I'm on my knees today Lord, with this one request. If it's true that it is not the absence of fear that makes us brave, but our mastery of it, would you make me a commander of mine? I wish to be constrained by fear no longer. I thank You.

The canvas was still stark white, but over the days it dissolved into warm colors, earth tones, burnt orange, brick red, mustard yellow. A woman eventually appeared with her back turned. She was in a desert, running toward the sun. You couldn't see her face, but she was wearing a flowing yellow dress, and the muscles in her calves were tight and strained. Her right wrist was dripping with blood, outstretched at the searing sunlight, begging it to stop.

On an afternoon in late July, Danni was painting, heard herself breathing so loud that it felt like someone was standing next to her now. Out of the corner of her eye, she checked. There was no one. She had been *that* engrossed.

She stepped back from the canvas, and "Whoa" was all she could say.

She looked at the portrait, felt it looking at her.

So much pain. Barefoot. Her feet blistered.

Danni dipped her brushes in the mayonnaise jar, watched the gray turn to brown, and went back to the yellow on her palette. She made the sun a bit brighter. There was still hope.

And when she was finished, the easel placed in her living

room, exactly where she wanted it, Danni surrounded it with all the stones.

. . .

"*Can I come* stay with you?"

"What?"

"You said call if I needed anything . . ."

"I know, but—"

"Just for a few days."

"What about summer school?"

"I got a C. Proud of me?"

"Of course I am, DeMarco."

"Ma said I could."

"Let me speak to her."

"Praise the Lord." Ma finally picked up after DeMarco had yelled her name several times. Danni couldn't believe she was actually home.

"Ma? You're home?"

"Oh, Lord." Ma sounded afraid. "What's wrong?"

"Nothing," Danni assured her. "DeMarco called asking if he could come stay with me for a while."

Ma exhaled. "That boy's gone worry me sick, bugging me about coming to stay with you."

"Well, he can," Danni said, "for a few days if he'd like."

"Uh-huh."

"You could use the break."

"Child, we've got work now, rest when we die."

"Maybe so, Ma."

Ma coughed, went to fumbling with what sounded like some pots and pans. "This kitchen's a mess. He's a handful, you know."

"I know it. So were we."

Ma laughed her husky laugh. "If you're willing to have him."

"I am."

"When!" DeMarco shouted, having listened on the extension.

"Saturday," Danni suggested. "Maybe a week."

Danni didn't have a lot of money, unemployment wasn't much. She certainly couldn't afford to buy him much while he was visiting, but Danni knew better than that. Her presence would be enough.

· · ·

Chantel Bess wanted to get right down to business. No sooner had Danni sat down in the office of the owner of Toledo's up-and-coming hot new gallery when, with laugh lines framing her cat eyes, she gestured at Danni's portfolio. "Let's take a look," she said.

And so Danni bared her most intimate reflection. Chantel studied that painting as if afterward she was going to have to take a quiz over what she'd seen. That made Danni nervous. That, and the fact that Chantel wasn't saying anything.

She looked up. "May I?" She gestured with her hand, wanting to touch.

"Sure," she replied.

Chantel's finger touched the sun, and she hummed an exhale. "It's so real," she said. "It's like if you touch it, you'll feel it. Even the blood on her feet."

Without looking up, Chantel continued, "You have such emphasis on strength. The muscles in her calves, they're worked so hard."

Danni sat up, peered over onto the desk, and realized that she had been right.

Chantel said, "You see?"

"Yeah," Danni agreed. They had worked so hard indeed.

Chantel said, "That is *very* moving." And though she still didn't look up, she proceeded with her comments. "You have a subtle flair for embellishment. It's real, but suspended from reality a bit, not so reflective, more interpretive. Almost fantastical. It's very distinct."

"Well, thank you."

She finally looked up at Danni, her eyes excited. "And what I would suggest is that you go even further with that as you continue with your career. It's the way *you* see the world, and it's fascinating. Your influence comes from within, it's apparent."

"Okay . . ." Danni had a questioning look on her face. What exactly was she suggesting?

Chantel closed Danni's portfolio, "We're really looking for that edge, an innovative appeal here."

"I see," Danni felt the heaviness of disappointment.

"Here's my card." Chantel gave it to her. "What we're currently planning is an extravaganza to begin the weekend after Thanksgiving, carry on through March. Each week, a different artist from across the country. We're looking for the best of the future."

"I see . . ."

"Check your schedule, get back to me once you do, let me know which week will be Danni Blair's week."

Danni's heart fluttered with joy. "Really?"

"We'll want to confirm a date, at least by Labor Day weekend. We'd want you to prepare a lecture. It'll be open to the public, of course, free. We might want to arrange a meet and greet with college students perhaps as well."

"I would *love* that."

"Well, then I guess I should also tell you that half the proceeds, if any of your pieces should sell, we've already promised to charity."

"I guess that means I've got to create something that's going to sell."

Chantel stood up, extended her hand. "I'll look forward to seeing what you create, to watching your career grow, Mrs. Blair."

"*Miss Blair,*" Danni corrected her.

• • •

Danni closed the freezer, pulled a spoon from the dishwasher, and took Ben & Jerry with her over to the couch. She stuck a spoonful of Mint Chocolate Cookie in her mouth, and almost tripped on one of those joysticks from that damn Nintendo, Game Cube, Sega, or whatever it was.

"I've told you about leaving these things all across the floor like this," she said to DeMarco.

"My bad." He was stretched out on the floor, flipping through the channels and settling in on ESPN. "You're eating ice cream for breakfast?"

She ignored him, stuck another big old spoonful in her mouth.

"How come I had to eat bacon and eggs?"

"Because I'm grown," she told him. "And you're not."

"Ain't fair."

"Can you please find something else to watch?"

"Every time I put it on sports . . . . dag. You used to like hoop."

"Don't you watch cartoons anymore?"

"Uh, hello, in two weeks I'll be a sophomore in high school. Remember?"

"Uh, and when I'm fifty-five years old I hope I'm still watching Bugs Bunny, so now."

He laughed, flipped through the stations some more.

"What's this," he asked.

On the screen was the entranceway into the building. Construction workers were putting in the new front door.

"That's the security monitor," she told him.

"Sweet!" He sat up. "You can watch people."

"Yup."

"It's like reality TV, right here in the building."

"It's for security."

"Ah, ha." He laughed. "Look at that dude's shorts. They look so gay."

The phone rang and Danni reached for it.

"Hey."

"Yes." Kizzy's voice was dry. "DeMarco please?"

Danni rolled her eyes and sat up. "Kizzy," she said, "De-Marco has been here two weeks. At what point are you gonna stop calling here acting like we're complete strangers. You can say hello to me too, you know."

"Hello."

"Kiz."

"What? I said hello."

Danni took one final spoonful and went back into the kitchen with the pint-size carton. She closed the freezer and sat on the counter. "All we've been through, Kiz, I think we should at least be able to catch up with one another every once in a while."

Kizzy replied, "I just called to speak to DeMarco, to see if he wanted to go to Cedar Point tomorrow. Mike's son will be in town, we're taking him."

"Mike? As in *busted-up-shoes-wearing* Mike?"

"Very funny."

"Mike who drives the Chevrolet Malibu?"

"Long as he's taking me somewhere in it. What."

"I bet."

"We're just testing the water."

"And . . . ?"

"I mean . . . I don't know. He's a nice guy. I never said he wasn't nice. We've just got some things we need to work on."

"I can't believe you're seeing Mike Lothery!"

"And I can't believe you haven't called me, bitch. I coulda been sick or anything."

"Well, you haven't called me either."

"Works both ways."

"Well," Danni said, "every time you call here you act like you can't speak. You started it."

"Danni."

"What?"

"We sound like some damn teenagers. You've been hanging out with DeMarco too long."

"So what's been up?"

"Not much. You?"

"About the same."

"I did try to call you once, at work. What happened?"

Danni hopped off the counter, opened the freezer again, and pulled Ben & Jerry right back out. "I got fired."

"You did?"

"I sure did."

"You cool?"

"No, but I will be," she said. "Actually, you know what, I am. I don't know when I'm gonna find another job, but I will. In the meantime, I'm cool."

"Yo!" DeMarco called from the living room.

"Yes, DeMarco." She held the phone away from her ear.

"Can we get a dog?"

"Sure," she replied. "You can win a stuffed one at Cedar Point tomorrow."

"Girl," Kizzy laughed. "Did I really just hear him ask if he could get a dog?"

"I'd like to see me try to feed him *and* a dog. Please."

"How is it, having him around?"

"He seems glad to be here. I have to stay on him about things, and I'm about ready to throw that boom box out the window though, but he's such a sweetheart overall . . ."

"Well," Kizzy said, "he's welcome over here anytime, if you ever need a break. You sure you're still gonna go ahead and keep him for the school year?"

"I wouldn't have it any other way. Someone did it for us."

DeMarco's voice was full of panic this time. *"Danni . . ."*

"What is it now, DeMarco? You see I'm on the phone."

"Uh-oh," he said. "You better come . . ."

Danni ran into the living room. "What?"

He was pointing at the television screen. Two men in white cargo suits were still working on the door. That was it.

"Okay, DeMarco. What?"

He was shaking his head. "I could've sworn I just saw D.L. came through the lobby."

"What?" Kizzy and Danni both said at the same time.

"He did," DeMarco insisted. "I swear. He had on a gray shirt, some gray silk-looking shorts, a gray baseball cap, a . . ."

Danni was running to the front door.

"Kizzy," she whispered as she looked out the peephole, watched the elevator. "DeMarco just said—"

"Girl, I know. I heard him."

DeMarco was standing next to Danni now in the doorway, trying to look out of the peephole as well.

"Oh, my goodness," Danni looked down at the ice cream-stained oversize Allen Iverson T-shirt she was wearing, her fluffy pink slippers. She felt her hair, still wrapped in the silk scarf from sleeping. "I look a hot mess!"

She heard the elevator open, and Danni wanted to cry. She shouldered the phone, put one hand over her mouth, and the other hand over DeMarco's.

"Girl, what's happening," Kizzy wanted to know.

And Dallas Laylock was right there, standing right there on the other side of the door. His head distorted, but Danni could tell that he was indeed rocking cornrows now. Still, he looked as handsome as ever. And he knocked.

DeMarco was giggling, trying to squirm out of Danni's grasp. She took her hand off his face, and made a fist.

She mouthed the words, "You bet not."

He covered his own mouth now, but a laugh was audible.

"Danni," Kizzy said. "You there? Is that him?"

Danni looked back out of the peephole. He knocked again.

"Oh my goodness," she whispered to Kizzy. "It's him. It's him. What should I do?"

"Girl, answer the damn door."

Danni whispered, "I can't let him see me like this. I'm looking a mess. You crazy?"

He knocked again.

Shit.

She pointed at DeMarco, gestured with her hand, lip-synced, told him to say that she wasn't there.

Dallas knocked some more, harder this time.

"Girl," Kizzy said. "He's gonna knock down that door, you better answer him."

Eff it.

Danni cleared her throat. "What?"

"Danni, it's me."

DeMarco reached up for the chain, and Danni slapped his hand. He cracked up laughing.

Dallas said, "Oh, you got company. It's cool."

"No," Danni said. "I mean yes." She changed her mind. None of his damn business who was over there.

"Girl," Kizzy said. "If you don't let that man in. I swear. I promise you. I'll . . . I don't even know what I'll call you, I'll have to invent some new words."

DeMarco reached up for the chain again.

And this time Danni let him. She folded her arms across her chest, was hoping to cover up the ice cream stain, but couldn't. Oh well. She wasn't trying to look good for him anyhow. Wasn't like he was her man.

DeMarco had it partially right. Dallas was wearing a gray silk suit.

Still, she got the tingles when she looked in his eyes.

"What's up?" DeMarco's eyes were lit as he held out his fist.

Dallas looked relieved, smiled, and gave DeMarco some dap. "Little man, how you doin'?"

"Dallas," Danni said. "You've heard me talk about DeMarco. He stays with me now, I guess you could say."

"Girl," Kizzy said. "Call me back when he leaves. Be nice."

"Okay, I will." Danni put the phone on the table.

DeMarco said, "S'up on the autograph, D.L.?"

"Sure, little man. Got a pen?"

And DeMarco zipped past them, was gone into his room.

He looked at her. She looked right back at him.

"You didn't call first," she reminded him.

"Danni."

"What?"

"Later for all that."

DeMarco returned with a basketball, a T-shirt, a piece of paper, and a big thick black permanent marker. Dallas signed every last one of the items, and even DeMarco's tennis shoes.

"Ay, Danni, can I—"

"Yes." She already knew what DeMarco was going to ask. "Just check back in with me."

He jetted out the door, was headed down to the ball court up the street.

"That was nice of you," Danni said.

"Anything for the kids," he replied.

"So what's up, stranger?"

"Man. I can't even front. It's good to see you."

She took a breath. "So what made you come by?"

"How've you been? You a'ight?"

"I'm okay."

"Hungry?"

"No, I'm not . . ."

"Nah, let me stop. I'm gettin' on a plane in about two hours."

"Well, good for you, Dallas. Handle your business."

"Shouldn't be gone but a day or two, though," he said.

"Well, have a safe trip."

"All right if I call you while I'm gone?"

"Because?"

"Better yet, how 'bout you come?"

"Are you nuts?" She laughed. "No."

"Come go. Bring lil' man. Florida, just for two days."

"I can't."

"Trippin'."

"Dallas, you think you can just walk in here and act like—"

He grinned. "Miss me?"

"Have a safe trip," she said happily.

"Yeah, all right."

She realized then that she was slouching, that her mood and her posture had both gotten pretty funky, and she hadn't meant for it to. She straightened back up. "How've you been?"

"Straight. What can I say?"

"I'm glad to hear it."

"I see you quit your job. I called there first."

"Actually, I got fired. But it's cool, hey."

"Is it?"

"I'll find something else eventually."

"If you want something, baby, you gotta go after it, act like you own it already." He looked like he wanted to say something, but he shook his head.

"What, Dallas? Something on your mind, spit it out."

"All that shit you was talkin', all that 'you're not ready to be the man I need you to be . . .'"

"Right."

"I feel that."

"Well, good."

"It's like my man Napoleon, a'ight? Check it. He said that 'Ability is nothing without opportunity' though. Feel me?"

"Dallas, you're always talking in riddles and rhymes, saying what somebody else said. Anybody can read a book and quote from it."

"A'ight." He took a step toward her.

She took a step back. "All right, what?"

He stood still. Took a deep breath. "No quotes."

"No quotes."

"Maybe I wasn't honest, but I never lied to you."

"Dallas, please. No loopholes."

"I'm try'n, baby."

"Dallas, two years, I took every blow, tried to love you the way you needed me to, and then, just . . ."

"You know what? I am selfish. You were damn right about that."

Danni may have even gasped out loud she was so surprised by his words.

He added, "But it's time-out. It's not all about Dallas Laylock, and I feel that. On the real. Some things you gotta learn the hard way, though, baby. Some things people can't tell you. Sometimes you've gotta lose something to appreciate having another chance."

This wasn't only about her, their relationship, Danni realized by the sadness in his voice. And so she asked him, "Are you okay?"

He bit his bottom lip.

She put her hands on her hips. "You know what, Dallas . . . ?"

His voice grew serious. "Not even listening to me, are you?"

"How's she?"

"How's who?"

"Yonnis Campbell, Dallas. You know who I'm talking about."

"How the hell should I know?"

"Yeah, right. She works for the team."

"For the Pistons."

"Exactly."

"So we gon' stand here and talk about her? Or we gon' deal with us?"

"Excuse me?" She tightened her arms.

"I'm not thinkin' about her, a'ight? I want you to come with me to Miami, be there when I sign."

"Please. You think you can just—"

"Let me finish," he interrupted. "You're not even hearin' me."

"Well, as far as I'm—"

"No, no, no." He held up his finger, shook his head. "Listen to me for a change."

She sat down on the dining-room chair, crossed one leg over the other, and grimaced when she saw her fluffy pink slippers. But, oh well. "Go ahead," she told him.

He pulled up the chair, sat on the opposite side of the table from her. "It's like this," he said.

"I'm listening."

"I met you . . ."

"Umm-hmm . . ."

"Dug you from the get-go. My round-the-way girl. Sassy but classy, know what I'm sayin'? Something about you. The way you spoke your mind. The way you demanded so much re-spect. That shit kinda turned me on, know what I'm sayin'?"

"Umm-hmm . . ."

"But that's the exact same thing that pisses me off about you. You never let up."

"Umm-hmmm . . ."

"I miss my baby's smile."

"Umm-hmm . . ."

"And I'm tired of not hearin' your voice."

"Umm-hmm . . ."

"Not seein' you in one of my shirts."

Danni clenched her teeth. She missed that, too.

He lowered his head for a moment, and when he looked up, a new strain and added sincerity was in his eyes. "I miss my baby."

She felt short of breath.

He got up from the table. "Come here," he said.

"No," she said.

He was standing in front of her now. "Just gon' leave me hangin' like this?"

She stood up, backed away. She stepped back some more, knocked the chair over. But she *kept* backing up.

And he waited.

She backed into the wall.

Checkmate.

He scratched the back of his neck, and went to her.

She shook her head.

He pressed his body up against hers, pressed her harder against the wall, his breathing heavy.

She reached up, to push him off her. But he grabbed her wrists, both with one hand, and he pinned her arms above her head. And she couldn't move. With his free hand he touched her lips, so gentle.

Pressing his forehead against the wall, he said, "Sometimes a man can't find the words . . ."

She closed her eyes, struggling to handle all her emotions from being unable to free herself.

He said, "I know I put you through some shit, but . . . I don't know what to say to get you to stop fighting," he said, squeezing her wrists even tighter.

"I don't know if I can do this, Dallas."

He kissed her forehead. "Me neither . . ."

"Dallas . . ."

"Come with me to Florida."

"Why? Because you're afraid of losing me? Or because you want me to come?"

"Both, gotdamnit."

"I've got DeMarco. I can't . . ."

"Bring lil' man too," he said. "Adjoining rooms and shit. It's two days. That's it."

"I don't know, I don't know . . ."

He kissed her cheek, tasted her tears. "I can't change shit that I did, baby, but I'm try'n to make this thing right."

"Dallas, I can't pretend like I feel safe without security."

"And I can't front like I can give it to you."

"So now what?"

He kissed her forehead. "I ain't never wanted to work this hard for something, not since the year I made the draft."

Danni inhaled, felt the wild twinges of fear in her chest, but then a long exhale relaxed her. "Miami, huh?"

"The Heat."

One more breath, and then a sigh. She said, "That'd be cool."

She felt his kisses on her other cheek, on her mouth, down her neck. And soon, she was kissing him back.

And it was so warm and familiar, their tongues expressing what neither one of them had been able to say for so long, but both still felt, more now than ever.

He managed to say amid their kisses, "I want us to find a house."

"Dallas," she said, "are you serious?"

"You know I don't say shit I don't mean." He kissed her again. "Anything for my baby."

And he let go of her wrists.

Her arms were free.

All of her was free.

She could walk away, run, if she wanted.

But she didn't. Their eyes locked. And she didn't look away.

She reached out, and he came back. She put her arms around his neck.

And she held him. And he held her back.

Surrender. Sweet, sweet surrender.

reading group guide

We hope that you have enjoyed *In the Paint* by Philana Marie Boles. The following questions are intended to facilitate your group's discussion of this sexy and provocative novel.

1. Throughout the novel, Danni reflects on her relationship with her foster mother and how it shaped her. How does this relationship affect her relationship with Dallas? How has it affected her views about religion?

2. Why is the title *In the Paint* suitable for this novel? How important is it for Dallas and Danni to be "in the paint"? What does being "in the paint" mean for each of them? How is being "in the paint" a state of mind?

3. Danni and Dallas have a roller-coaster ride with their love life throughout the novel. Do you agree with Danni's decision to take him back at the end? Do you think their relationship will be different than it was before? Why or why not?

4. A large part of this novel is about forgiveness—forgiving yourself as well as forgiving others. What is Danni's idea of forgiveness? Why is she afraid to forgive?

5. How do Dallas and Danni play games with one another in the novel? Who finally wins in the end?

6. Kizzy and Danni have different views on men and relationships. What is Kizzy's view? What is Danni's? Do their

views stay the same throughout the novel? How do their views change?

7. Boles has written several strong female characters into this novel, including Kizzy, Danni's mother, N'Drea, and Sage. Discuss the different relationships that Danni has with each of these women. What dynamics of women do these characters represent?

8. How is Roman Bilal a catalyst for change in Danni's life? What does his marriage to Sage teach her about love and redemption?

9. At one point, Danni remarks, "Not everything that hurts is bad, just as sure as not everything that feels good is right. Sometimes hurting, if it leads us to a better place, is a good thing." How does this quote apply to Danni?

10. This novel is about different types of relationships—relationships between men and women, mothers and daughters, friends, and family members. Which relationships does Danni cherish the most? How do you know?

11. At the end of the novel, Danni prays to be "constrained by fear no longer." How is Danni constrained by fear in the novel? Who else is ruled by fear?

12. Compare and contrast the woman that Danni is at the beginning of the novel to the woman that she is at the end. How has she changed? How has she stayed the same?